"Colonel! You should take a look at this."

The guard led them outside St. Basil's Cathedral and over to one of the trash cans in Red Square. He pointed inside the mouth of the barrel.

Sitting on some discarded trash was a woman's hand.

Goshenko reached in and pulled it out, which caused the captain of the guard to recoil. But the hand wasn't flesh and blood. It was stone. The stone hand of the Virgin Mother.

The colonel looked at it for a moment and then held it up so Danislov could see its hollow center. "I want to know what was hidden inside here, Sergeant. I don't care what you have to do, just get me whatever it was."

"Understood, sir."

"The American, Annja Creed, and her companion are staying over at the Marriott on Tverskaya Street." Colonel Goshenko nodded, satisfied. "I suggest you start there."

Titles in this series:

ROGUE Angel

Alex Archer

LIBRARY OF GOLD

A GOLD EAGLE BOOK FROM
W❂RLDWIDE®

TORONTO • NEW YORK • LONDON
AMSTERDAM • PARIS • SYDNEY • HAMBURG
STOCKHOLM • ATHENS • TOKYO • MILAN
MADRID • WARSAW • BUDAPEST • AUCKLAND

Recycling programs
for this product may
not exist in your area.

First edition July 2012

ISBN-13: 978-0-373-62157-6

LIBRARY OF GOLD

Special thanks and acknowledgment to
Joe Nassise for his contribution to this work.

Printed in U.S.A.

The
LEGEND

...THE ENGLISH COMMANDER TOOK
JOAN'S SWORD AND RAISED IT HIGH.

The broadsword, plain and unadorned,
gleamed in the firelight. He put the tip against
the ground and his foot at the center of the blade.
The broadsword shattered, fragments falling
into the mud. The crowd surged forward,
peasant and soldier, and snatched the shards
from the trampled mud. The commander tossed
the hilt deep into the crowd.
Smoke almost obscured Joan, but she continued
praying till the end, until finally the flames climbed
her body and she sagged against the restraints.

Joan of Arc died that fateful day in France,
but her legend and sword are reborn....

1

Footsteps in the dark.

That's all Ridolfo di Fioravanti heard at first, the tramp of booted feet somewhere in the distance, but it was enough. Though he couldn't see them yet, he knew who was marching down the long, dark tunnels toward him and the rest of the men working on the project. He knew that when they were at last revealed in the light of the oil lamps there would be no doubt of their intentions.

He had begun to suspect what was being prepared for them when the guards changed. For weeks the work crews had been accompanied by a squad of soldiers, there, he suspected, to prevent the workers from making off with the tools more than anything else. But within the past week the soldiers had been replaced by men wearing the black uniform and dog's head insignia of the Oprichniki, the czar's secret police. This was not a good sign. The Oprichniki were nothing more than sadistic thugs in uniform, brought into being to help the czar quell internal resistance and turned loose to terrorize and torture anyone he saw as a threat.

Ridolfo should have seen it coming. When Czar Ivan had first summoned him to his palace and told him what he wanted to do, Ridolfo had been too caught up in the technicalities of the project to see the danger. He'd let his excitement overcome his good sense and now it seemed he was going to pay for that oversight.

But not before he saw to his family's welfare.

He crossed the room to where his nephew, Giuseppe, was helping some of the other workers pile debris from an earlier excavation into a cart. Grabbing the boy by the arm, Ridolfo led him off to one side.

"I need you to take a message to your father for me," he told the boy.

"Now?"

"Yes, now."

"But I'll miss the end of the shift!"

The conditions they were working in were arduous, at best, and for a moment Ridolfo didn't understand why the boy would want to be slaving down here when he could be out in the sunlight above. But then the meaning of the boy's statement filtered past Ridolfo's fear enough to make sense. The workers were paid at the end of each work period. If Giu-

seppe left now, he'd forfeit the effort he'd put in up to this point.

If he doesn't leave now, he'll be dead.

"I will collect your wages myself," Ridolfo told him with a smile on his face. "Have no fear."

Ridolfo was the chief foreman and designer of the project, which made the lie seem convincing. Thankfully the boy took it at face value.

Ridolfo reached inside his shirt and removed the slim leather journal he kept secreted there. He passed it to Giuseppe.

"Take this to your father and tell him the crows are flying. Understand? The crows are flying."

Giuseppe frowned but nodded, anyway. "The crows are flying. Yes, sir."

"Good boy!" Ridolfo kept the smile on his face, but inside he wanted to scream. The sound of booted feet was much closer now and they were all but out of time. If the czar had sent his uniformed lapdogs down the emergency exit, they were already too late.

Only one way to find out...

"Come," he said with fake cheer, pulling his nephew into the rear section of the vault to where the narrow mouth of the emergency exit was half-hidden in the shadows. He stuck his head inside the tunnel and listened for as long as he dared, but didn't hear anything. Perhaps the way was still open.

He picked up the emergency lantern that always stood inside the entrance of the tunnel and lit it, il-

luminating the passageway before him. "This will take you directly to the surface," he said to the boy. "Better yet, by going this way you won't have to deal with the guards at the main entrance."

That last brought a smile to Giuseppe's face; he hated the dimwitted brutes that passed as guards around here. He took the lantern Ridolfo passed to him and, without a backward glance, scampered up the tunnel with the journal clutched in his other hand.

Ridolfo watched until the lantern's light disappeared around a bend and then he quickly moved away from the opening, not wanting to give those who were coming any indication that the passageway was in use. He'd worked out the plan with his brother several days ago when he'd first begun to suspect the end that Czar Ivan had in mind for those working on the project. The message was innocuous enough that it wouldn't raise concerns if the boy was caught and forced to disclose it, but Ridolfo's brother would understand what it meant. As any peasant knew, the only time the crows gathered was when they had something to feast upon.

Ridolfo stepped back into the main vault at the same time a squad of Oprichniki soldiers marched into the room, their weapons in hand, pointed toward the workers. The sight infuriated Ridolfo—how dare they threaten his men? But the angry shout that rose in his throat was instantly stifled when the tall, dark form of Ivan Vasilyevich IV, Grand Prince of Mos-

cow and Czar of the Russian Empire, also known as
Ivan the Terrible, stepped from behind the squad.

Ridolfo sank to one knee and his men followed
suit, none of them daring to look in the czar's direction. Ivan had been known to fly into a rage at even
an unintended slight.

Today, however, he seemed to be in a jovial mood.

"Get up!" came his deep, booming voice. "Get up!
The floor is no place for my chief architect."

Ridolfo did as he was told, still mindful that the
Oprichniki had not relaxed their watchfulness.

Ivan was tall, with wide shoulders and a broad
chest, made all the more intimidating by his seeming
boundless energy. He would never be called hand-
some, for his small eyes and hooked nose gave him
a sinister expression even when he was smiling, as
he was now.

"The work goes well, no?" he asked, his voice
made louder by the way it echoed off the close stone
walls.

Ridolfo nodded. "It does, indeed, Your Highness,"
he replied, surprised at his steadiness. He knew what
was coming, could see it in the gleam in the czar's
eyes, but he'd be damned if he let his fear overwhelm
him. He would play his part to the very end. Every
second he kept the czar occupied here was another
that his family could use to make their escape. "A
few more days and we should be complete."

The czar's joviality, of course, was a front. Upon

hearing the answer to his question, it quickly vanished, to be replaced by a deep frown. "Days?" The czar glanced with a heavy scowl at Nikolaevich, one of the men in the work crew, who swiftly turned his face away.

You bastard! Ridolfo thought at the revelation of the traitor, but he was careful to keep his expression neutral. He'd known the czar had spies in his work crew, but he'd never even suspected the big Muscovite.

Nothing to be done about it now.

"It is nothing vital," he said easily, trying to keep Ivan's legendary temper from erupting upon them all. "Cosmetic issues only."

The minute he said it, Ridolfo realized it was the wrong statement to make. The vault had not been designed for the public, but to protect Ivan's most precious treasure. A few rough spots here and there were nothing compared to keeping the secret of the vault's existence.

The self-satisfied smirk that flashed across the czar's face, there and gone again so quickly Ridolfo might have missed it if he wasn't looking intently, told the architect it was too late to try to fix the mistake.

He'd just killed his only opportunity to delay the inevitable. Ridolfo would not be leaving this chamber alive.

That realization brought with it a strange sense of

relief. There was no longer any need to worry about what was to happen; it was too late for that. With his death only moments away, he felt a surge of defiance, the likes of which he'd never felt before. As the other men in the work crew watched in surprise, Ridolfo slowly climbed to his feet, staring at the czar, letting the contempt he felt show plainly on his face.

Unfortunately, that contempt, righteous or not, was wasted on a murderous thug like Ivan the Terrible. The czar stepped back behind the circle of soldiers he'd brought with him and said clearly enough for everyone to hear, "Get rid of them, Captain. Every last one of them."

Ridolfo and his men were horribly outnumbered, but that didn't stop him and several of the other more perceptive workers from snatching up shovels and pickaxes and charging the hated Oprichniki with murder in their hearts.

The end result was all but preordained. Ridolfo managed to deliver a couple of blows with the pickax before the soldier in front of him parried a strike and thrust a thick-bladed cavalry sabre through Ridolfo's chest.

As the Italian architect lay bleeding to death on the cold stone tile his men had laid only days before, his last thought was of his brother's son and the clues buried in the pages of the journal the boy carried to the sunlight high above.

2

"You sounded a little tired in that one, Annja. Let's redo it, all right?"

Annja Creed stared out through the glass of the sound booth at the smiling face of her producer, Doug Morrell, and had to resist the urge to run him through with her sword. She sounded tired because she *was* tired; they'd been at this for more than nine hours already! If he wanted her to sound fresh and energetic, they were going to have to call it quits soon or she wouldn't have a voice left for tomorrow's session.

Annja worked as one of the hosts of *Chasing History's Monsters,* a cable television show that featured a combination of history crossed with the weird and unexplained. It was her job to act as the show's resident skeptic, using reason and history to explain some of the more fantastical ideas that were raised during each episode. It was a position she was well suited for. Her background as an archaeologist gave her the skills to examine disparate pieces of information and pull them together into logical theories, while her ability to speak multiple languages, specifically French, Spanish, Portuguese, Italian and Latin, allowed her to be comfortable in the foreign locations where the show often sent her.

Of course, her travel had a tendency to bring her face-to-face with all kinds of other trouble, as well. It was almost as if the sword were orchestrating her movements, causing her to be in the right place at the right time to defend the innocent and right wrongs. She'd faced off against enemies of all kinds since taking up the sword, from Thuggee death cults to the angry spirit of an ancient Inuit god. She never knew what she would be facing next.

The ancient Chinese used to curse people with the expression "May you live in interesting times." Since the sword came into her life, Annja understood the power in that curse.

Her life had certainly become interesting.

She'd arrived at the show's Manhattan studio early to get a jump on the voice-over work she was scheduled to do for the next three days. The powers-that-be had decided a *Chasing History's Monsters* boxed set was just the thing to help kick DVD sales up the charts. They wanted Annja to provide additional detail on the things she'd seen and heard while filming each episode. A kind of director's cut track, if you will, but from the host's perspective. The past week had been spent reviewing the episodes, making notes and then turning those notes into coherent remarks to be recorded during the voice-over sessions. Trying to reconstruct thought processes and research of the past several seasons' worth of programs hadn't been easy.

It had also stirred up plenty of other memories, as well. Her first encounter with Roux, meeting Garin Braden, the mystical reforging of the sword once carried by Joan of Arc, the new role she'd adopted as protector of the innocent and defender of the good. Her life had been put in danger more times than she could count. And yet she wouldn't trade it for the world. Somewhere, deep inside, she knew she'd been born to wield that sword. And she had every intention of doing so well into the foreseeable future. Even if she didn't understand the hows and whys behind it.

"Earth to Annja? Hellooo? Anybody home?"

Doug's voice over her headphones startled her from her reminiscing.

"I'm here, Doug. Just rehearsing the lines in my head. One more time and then I'm done for the night."

Doug's boyish grin flashed from the other side of the glass. "Sure, Annja, one more time and that's it."

It took them two more takes, actually, but when they were finished everyone involved applauded. It had been a long day, but they might be able to cut it down to two days if they kept this pace up.

Afterward Doug dragged Annja to his office to deliver his suggestions for what she should say during tomorrow's commentary.

As usual, he was way over the top.

"Not a chance, Doug," she found herself saying not five minutes after entering the room. "No way."

"But it will drive ratings through the roof, Annja!"

"I don't care if it blows them into outer space. I'm not going to say I witnessed a chupacabra attack outside Mexico City."

"Okay, forget the attack. How about just claiming you saw one? That should achieve the same effect."

"Yeah, of making me look like the world's biggest idiot. No, Doug, no chupacabra. Period."

"Now you're just being difficult."

"No, I'm being honest."

"Honest? Since when is that—?"

Thankfully Doug was interrupted by a knock at the door. A young brunette stuck her head inside the room.

"Mr. Morrell?"

Doug held up a finger to Annja as if to say, *Hold that thought* and then turned to face their visitor.

"Yes, Jessica?"

"This was just delivered for Annja," she said, handing him a fancy envelope tied with a red ribbon.

Annja couldn't miss the flirtatious smile Jessica sent

Doug, especially since the show's newest intern didn't even bother to glance in her direction. The look of irritation that crossed the girl's face when Doug distractedly took the envelope didn't go unnoticed, either. Neither did the way she shut the door too hard in her wake.

Annja stared at the closed door a moment, then turned to Doug and asked, "Why are you Mr. Morrell and I'm just plain old Annja?"

"Because you're the star of the show."

"Exactly. Shouldn't that be worth a little more respect?"

Doug shook his head. "Not when I'm the one paying her."

That was, she had to admit, a good point. Putting aside office politics for the moment, she turned her attention to the envelope Doug handed to her.

It was made from a thick, richly textured creamy paper that practically shouted money the minute she laid her hands on it. The ribbon was a classy affair, as well—a wide swatch of red velvet tied in an intricate bow. Untying it, she laid it aside, opened the envelope and withdrew a small white card.

Sir Charles Davies requests the honor of your company for dinner this evening. Gascogne, 7:00 p.m.

There was a phone number underneath for her to RSVP.

Annja sighed. After working all day on the voiceovers, all she wanted to do was to go home and relax. Maybe grab some dark chocolate and red wine, then lounge in the bath. She certainly didn't have the energy to be out entertaining someone she didn't know, especially someone with the stature and notoriety of Sir Charles.

"Sorry, not tonight." She dropped the invitation into the trash can next to Doug's desk.

Doug, of course, freaked.

"Are you insane?" He snatched the card out of the trash and thrust it back at her. "You have to go!"

Annja put her hands behind her back, refusing to take it. "I don't have to go. And I don't want to."

Doug stared at her in horror and disbelief. "But… it's Sir Charles!" he sputtered.

"So?"

She didn't care if it was the Queen of England. She was tired and didn't want to spend the evening trying to be gracious and putting on a show. And what kind of notice was that? A few hours? He could at least have had the decency to plan in advance.

Doug clearly disagreed and, in fact, looked ready to pull his hair out.

"So?" He brandished the invitation in front of him like an exhibit in a court of law. "So? You're not talking about some fan off the street, Annja. This is Sir Charles, one of the richest men in America, for heaven's sake."

Actually, one of the richest men in the world, she

thought to herself. She didn't dare say it aloud, however, knowing it would just fuel Doug's argument. Davies hung around with men the likes of Carlos Slim, Bill Gates and Warren Buffett—self-made billionaires who could do anything they ever wanted to given the vast size of their personal fortunes.

She was a little curious, she had to admit. It wasn't every day a man like Davies came knocking on her door and she found herself wondering just what it was he wanted from her.

Doug took a deep breath and visibly calmed himself.

"Think about this for a minute, Annja. What show do you work for?"

"Chasing History's Monsters."

"Uh-huh. And what channel airs that program?" he asked in an exaggeratedly patient tone, like a parent talking to a slow-witted child.

Annja didn't care for it. "You know well enough what cable channel we're on, Doug."

He acted as if he hadn't heard her. "I'm sorry, what channel was that again?"

Annja glared at him for a long moment. Doug could be as stubborn as she could at times.

But he wasn't about to budge.

He finally flashed a phony smile at her. "Now here's the big one, Annja. Who owns the network that airs our little cable TV program?"

She didn't even have to think about it. She saw the

name every time she cashed one of her paychecks. None other than Sir Charles Davies.

The invitation had come from her boss's boss's boss. Which meant she could no more ignore it than she could sprout wings and fly on command.

"Damn."

"Exactly!"

Grinning in triumph, Doug picked up the phone on his desk, dialed a number. When it was answered, he said, "This is Doug Morrell, executive producer of *Chasing History's Monsters.* Please inform Sir Charles that Miss Creed would be more than happy to join him for dinner this evening."

He listened for a moment, jotted something down on a piece of paper and then said, "Excellent. She'll be expecting you," before hanging up.

Annja was not happy with the situation, not at all. "Why don't you go in my place?" she suggested.

"He didn't invite me. He invited you." He frowned as he said it and Annja abruptly realized that he was actually jealous of her. While she was content being a cohost for the show, Doug had ambitions of moving up the corporate hierarchy, perhaps spinning off a few program ideas of his own. A meeting with Sir Charles was the kind of thing that could change a career overnight.

For just a moment she debated asking him to accompany her for the evening, but decided against it. As much as she'd welcome the company, Sir Charles probably wouldn't appreciate someone unexpected crashing that party.

Again, she found herself wondering what Davies wanted. Given what she knew about him, she couldn't picture him even watching the show, never mind being one of her fans. Which meant it had to do with some other aspect of her life. She'd been approached by rich individuals and organizations in the past, usually to investigate the provenance of a particular collection or item, so perhaps that was it.

Heaven forbid it had anything to do with a new position at the network. Her current role left her time to pursue her first love, archaeology, while responding to the call of the sword.

Only one way to find out.

Doug handed her the piece of paper with a phone number on it. "Sir Charles is sending a driver to pick you up at your loft in Brooklyn at six. Call that number if you're running late. And please, Annja, best behavior while you're with him. Don't say or do anything rash."

An impish grin crossed her face. "Doug. You wound me. Would I do anything like that?"

The sour expression that crossed his face was answer enough.

She was still laughing as she headed out the door.

3

Having resigned herself to going, Annja decided that she'd pull out all the stops and at least wear something nice. She took a sleek black dress out of the back of her closet, trying but ultimately failing to remember the last time she'd worn it, which said something entirely too depressing about her social life. She brought it to the bathroom with her, showered, dried off and put it on, pleased that the dress still fit.

The limo arrived promptly at six, as expected. Annja had seen it coming down the street and was just stepping out of her building as it rolled to a stop outside. The driver, a large man in a chauffeur's uniform, held the door for her while she slipped inside, smoothing her dress over her legs.

Gascogne, the restaurant Sir Charles had chosen for their meeting, was on Eighth Avenue in Manhattan's Chelsea District. Normally the traffic on a Friday night would make it next to impossible to get from her flat in Brooklyn and into the city in anything less than an hour, but the driver knew his job and he maneuvered the limo through the crush of traffic like a shark through a school of tuna. He had her at the door of the restaurant with ten minutes to spare.

There was a small line outside waiting for tables and Annja drew more than a few admiring stares as she emerged from the limousine. She was escorted inside by the waiting maître d'.

The restaurant had the ambience of a French bistro, with cream-colored walls, white linen tablecloths and muted lighting. It was artfully done and Annja knew that what looked effortless had probably been damned difficult to pull off.

Transferred to a waiter, she was led across the room toward a table in the back corner where Sir Charles—she recognized him from all the media coverage—sat waiting for her. He was alone, which surprised her. She'd expected either a private dining room or bodyguards. He was, after all, one of the richest men in the world, which would make him a target nine ways from Sunday.

She was getting closer to the table, and still puzzling it over, when she noticed a couple seated at a nearby table. The woman wore a finely tailored suit and Annja might not have seen the telltale bulge of what could only be a gun holstered beneath the woman's arm if she hadn't stretched to reach the saltshaker.

And just like that it was easy to pick out Sir Charles's crew from the rest of the restaurant patrons. A pair of men in business suits a few tables over kept looking around the room a little too regularly, and a slightly older man drinking at the bar had been watching her in the mirror ever since she'd entered.

That Sir Charles wasn't alone was oddly reassuring and she relaxed as she joined him at the table.

He greeted her warmly, extending his hand across the table for her to shake rather than getting up out of his chair. Annja wasn't surprised or offended; an auto accident had robbed him of the use of his lower body more than two decades before. And if she hadn't known, his wheelchair would have been a dead giveaway. He'd been a tall, broad-shouldered man before the accident and had managed to retain much of his physique in the years since. He had a crushing grip and a wide smile.

"Ah, Miss Creed. Wonderful to see you!"

As the waiter held her chair for her, Davies paused to let her settle in.

"Something to drink, mademoiselle?" the waiter asked in French, and was nonplussed when she immediately responded in the same language, selecting a glass of pinot grigio. It had been some time since she'd been out for a nice dinner. She was going to take advantage of the situation and enjoy herself.

Davies's blue eyes were sparkling. "Thank you for agreeing to meet with me on such short notice. I'm only in the city for the evening and didn't want to miss the opportunity."

Despite her earlier thoughts, Annja felt herself swayed by his charm. "It's my pleasure, Sir Charles."

The elderly man waved his hand as if shooing away a bad odor. "Please. Charles is fine. I reserve that Sir Charles stuff for those I don't particularly care for all that much."

Annja laughed. "I think I like you already. Okay, Charles it is."

The waiter brought their drinks—the wine for Annja and a refill of what looked like Scotch for Charles. He waited until the server was out of earshot before continuing.

"A mutual friend of ours in Paris said you might be able to help with a particular problem I'd like to solve."

Annja only had one friend in Paris who could possibly run in the same social circles as Davies and that was Roux. Incredibly wealthy in his own right, perhaps even more wealthy than Charles Davies, Roux was unlike any other man she'd ever met. Save one.

He'd lived for more than five hundred years, which probably had something to do with that, she thought.

Roux had been an instrumental force in her life for years now. She had been with him when she'd discovered the final missing piece to the shattered sword that had once been wielded by Joan of Arc. Annja had been in Roux's study with him when the blade had mystically reforged itself right before their very eyes and, by Annja's way of thinking, had chosen her to be its next bearer. Since then Roux had become a kind of mentor to her, sharing what he knew of the blade and its purpose.

Which made sense given that the blade had had a significant impact on his life, as well.

He'd been Joan's protector, charged with delivering her safely back behind French lines, a job he'd ultimately failed to do. Joan had been captured and, vastly outnumbered, he and his young apprentice, Garin Braden, had been unable to do anything but stand and watch as the English soldiers burned her at the stake for witchcraft and heresy. Joan's sword had been shattered by the commander in charge of the execution detail, the pieces quickly gathered up by onlookers as souvenirs. It was only later that Roux discovered how his failure to live up to his vow to protect the young maiden had changed him and, by extension, his apprentice, as well. The two men stopped aging, appearing today just as they did five centuries before. Determined to be the master of his own fate, Roux had set out on a quest to reunite the shattered pieces of Joan's sword, thinking that restoring the weapon might somehow end the curse.

Unfortunately, this brought him into rivalry with

his former apprentice, Garin, who decided that he was quite happy living forever and didn't see it as a curse at all. Because he saw the restoration of the blade as an attempt to undo the very act that had granted them an ageless life in the first place, Garin spent the next couple hundred years trying to kill Roux whenever he got the chance. It was only recently, when the blade had been reformed without any harm coming to them, that the two men had put aside their conflict and begun to cooperate.

Roux had sent customers her way on several occasions and so Annja wasn't exactly surprised to hear of his recommendation.

"And how is the stubborn old goat?" she asked.

"As willful as ever," Davis replied, "and determined to make everyone around him well aware of it."

Their meal came, sea bass for Charles and a sirloin for Annja, and they spent the next thirty minutes enjoying the food and talking about inconsequential things. Once the table had been cleared and coffee ordered, Charles finally got down to business.

"What can you tell me about the Library of Gold?" he asked.

Annja didn't even need to think about it. The library was one of the great unsolved mysteries of the archaeological world and she was well-versed in its history.

"It's a collection of ancient books gathered over

several hundred years by the Byzantine Empire and collected in the library at Constantinople. It supposedly included roughly eight hundred books written in Greek, Latin, Hebrew and Arabic, including some exceedingly rare volumes as a complete set of the "History of Rome" by Titus Livius, poems by Kalvos, "The Twelve Caesars" by Suetonius and individual works by Virgil, Aristophanes, Polybius, Pindar, Tacitus and Cicero."

Annja took a sip of her wine, warming to the subject. "Many of the books would have been written by hand, which, if they surfaced on today's market, would make them incredibly valuable. Never mind the several hundred editions that were supposedly created specifically for the various emperors, which were rumored to have had their covers inlaid with gold and encrusted with jewels of all shapes and sizes.

"When the emperor's niece, Sophia Palaeologus, married the Grand Prince of Moscow, Ivan III, she took the library with her back to Russia. Reasons for this vary. Some say it was a part of her marriage dowry, while others insist that it was to keep the library from falling into the hands of Sultan Mahomet II, who was threatening Constantinople at the time. Either way it turned out to be fortuitous, because the sultan's forces eventually sacked Constantinople. I guess in the end it really doesn't matter. The library went to Russia and that pretty much sealed its doom."

Charles was watching her closely, sizing her up it seemed. "Why's that?" he asked.

"The difference in the cities themselves, for one. At the time, most of the buildings in Moscow were made of wood. Fires were frequent, the dry air leeching the moisture out of the wood in the summertime and causing them to burn fast. A small one-building fire could engulf an entire section of the city if it wasn't quickly contained. Compare that with Constantinople, which was far older than Moscow and where most of the buildings were of cut stone. For this reason alone, the library was safer in Constantinople.

"Sophia apparently came to the same conclusion. Soon after arriving in Moscow, she convinced her new husband to rebuild the entire Kremlin, replacing the wooden structures with buildings of brick and stone. The library was moved to the Temple of the Nativity of the Theotokos and that's where it remained until Sophia's stepson, Ivan IV, came to power in 1533."

"That hardly sounds like doom and gloom," Charles said skeptically.

Annja smiled. "The library passed into the hands of Ivan IV, also known as Ivan the Terrible and the Butcher of Novgorod. This is the same man who killed his own son and heir in a fit of rage by striking him repeatedly over the head with an iron rod. He created a secret police force that was actively encouraged to rape, loot, torture and kill in his name to keep the populace under control. Does that sound like the kind of man priceless texts should be entrusted to?"

Charles grimaced and shook his head.

Annja went on. "Recognizing the potential danger the library was in, the Vatican tried to purchase it outright from the self-declared czar. Ivan refused. Afraid his enemies would try to take it from him by force, Ivan hired an Italian architect named Ridolfo di Fioravanti to design and build a secret vault to house the library. Months into the project Fioravanti and the library both vanished."

"So what do you think happened to it?" Charles asked casually.

Annja thought about that one for a moment, then shrugged. "I don't have a clue," she said. "And given what's gone on over there for the past century or so, we'll probably never know."

Charles leaned toward her, his eyes shining with excitement. "What would you say if I told you I knew where it was? Or, at least, had direct information that could lead you to it?"

Annja laughed. "If I had a nickel for every time someone told me they knew where to find a long-lost treasure, I'd be as rich as you are, Charles."

He stared at her and then lifted his hand. The woman Annja had noticed earlier immediately got up and walked over. She nodded once at Annja, then slid a manila envelope into her boss's hands before returning to her seat.

Charles put the envelope down on the table in front of him and folded his hands over it.

Annja couldn't take her eyes off it. Her heart was racing with the same electric excitement she felt just before entering a lost tomb. When at last she tore her gaze away, she found Charles watching her with a wry grin.

"Last month I was approached by a young man named Gianni Travino, who claimed to be a descendent of the architect hired to build Ivan's secret vault. After establishing that he was who he claimed to be, and that his family was, indeed, distantly related to Fioravanti himself, Gianni and I had a long chat."

Charles paused and glanced around, and Annja realized it was all part of the show. Her host apparently loved a good story and he was milking this one for all it was worth.

That was fine with Annja. She was as much a romantic when it came to a mystery as anyone else. Perhaps even more so, given what she did for a living. She settled back and let Charles tell it his way.

"Gianni's father passed away a few months ago and while going through the old man's things, Gianni discovered a hand-carved wooden box that no one in the family remembered having seen before. None of his father's keys fit the lock, so Gianni took it to a locksmith and had it opened. Inside he found a leather journal he claims was not only written by Fioravanti himself, but that also holds the key to finding the secret resting place of the Library of Gold."

Annja could guess where this was going, as she'd heard stories like it a hundred times before. Charles was going to ask her to use the journal to track down the treasure and would offer some percentage of whatever they recovered in payment for her time and energy. She almost stopped him right then and there. But he'd invited her out for an expensive night on the town, something that didn't happen all that often, and treated her with respect. A little courtesy wouldn't cost her anything but a bit of time, and she had enough of that to go around at the moment.

Charles Davies surprised her. "As you can imagine, I was immediately skeptical," he said. "I mean, come on, Fioravanti's journal suddenly shows up after being hidden away in a wooden box in some old guy's closet for the past four hundred years? Seriously?"

Annja laughed. Charles was well into his sixties and hearing him use language more suitable for someone a quarter his age struck her as highly amusing. Never mind the fact that he was calling someone else an "old guy."

"I see you understand my skepticism," he said with a twinkle in his eye. "That's why I asked Mr. Travino to allow me to examine the journal and make a determination as to its authenticity on my own. Surprisingly, he was happy to let me."

"And?"

Rather than answer her, Charles simply pushed the envelope in her direction.

Inside was a report from the office of David Carmichael, the chief archivist at the Smithsonian Institution in Washington, D.C. Annja had never met Carmichael, but she was familiar with his work and knew that you weren't put in charge of the country's historical records if you were sloppy with your science.

She turned the report to catch more light and began reading. It didn't take her long to get the impact of what the document was saying.

Charles had sent the journal to Carmichael with the request that he do what he could to verify the historical provenance of the document. He'd supplied written permission from Gianni to run whatever tests were necessary, paid the required fees to cover the costs and included a generous contribution to the Smithsonian's general fund in exchange for moving the project to the front of the line.

It had still taken two months, but that was far better than the three-year wait Annja knew it could have been.

The results were far from expected.

Glancing through the report and the accompanying documentation relative to the tests themselves, it was clear Carmichael had put the journal through the ringer. He'd tested the composition of the paper, ink, glue and leather cover, verifying that they were all produced somewhere between 1500 and 1550, which was smack in the middle of the time frame necessary for it to be authentic. Annja knew this wasn't proof of the journal's authenticity in and of itself. A good forger will use age-appropriate materials when assembling a forgery intended to pass close scrutiny, but at least it was a start.

As expected, Carmichael put the journal through other rounds of tests, such as examining the way the words were inscribed on the page as well as the language used within the text. He verified that the word usage and syllogisms were all appropriate to the time period in question.

His final conclusion?

While he couldn't say for certain the journal had been written by Ridolfo di Fioravanti, Carmichael did confirm it had mostly likely been assembled in the mid-1500s in southern Italy and that the ink that was used to inscribe the text on its pages was of the type available in Russia during the same time period.

It was pretty solid support for Gianni and his story, as far-fetched as it might seem.

Annja slipped the report back into the envelope and passed it across the table to Charles. "I want to see it for myself."

He smiled. "I was hoping you would say that."

4

Sir Charles Davies had a house outside the city in Greenwich, just across the Connecticut state line, and it was there Annja found herself early the next morning. She'd wanted to see the journal for herself before listening to the rest of Charles's proposal and he'd readily agreed. Doug hadn't been so thrilled when she'd called to let him know she wasn't going to make the day's voice-over session.

"We've still got a ton of work ahead of us, Annja. We can't afford to take a day off."

"And yet that's exactly what we're going to do," she said with a mischievous grin. "Unless, of course, you want me to tell Sir Charles I couldn't possibly continue the discussion we started last night about his funding an expedition to find the lost library of Ivan the Great."

"We can't afford to waste any more...wait. Did you say Ivan the Great?"

"I did, but you're right. We couldn't possibly take a day off. I'll tell Sir Charles I can't make it and…"

"Wait!" Doug cried, a hint of panic in his voice. "You can't tell him that."

"But I thought you wanted—"

"Never mind what you thought. I'm telling you I want you to spend whatever time you need with Sir Charles. Make that expedition a reality and make sure you get broadcast rights for *Chasing History's Monsters*."

Annja had barely been able to keep herself from laughing as she'd solemnly agreed to follow Doug's instructions to the letter before she hung up the phone.

She'd taken a taxi from the Greenwich train station and now stood outside the property's gates, staring at the mansion just beyond. The place was enormous; at least as expansive as Roux's place outside Paris.

Well, you knew Charles had money, right? Just what did you expect?

Definitely not this.

She was reaching for the intercom when the gates swung silently open. Clearly, someone had been watching the closed-circuit security cameras for her arrival. She glanced up at the black eye of the camera pointed at her from on top of the nearby gatepost, gave it a little wave and headed up the drive toward the front door.

Charles was waiting there in his wheelchair, a smile on his face. Next to him stood a good-looking man in his late twenties, with a mop of curly brown hair and big brown eyes. He was dressed in jeans and a button-down Oxford, Italian loafers on his feet.

This must be Gianni.

"Annja, so glad you could make it," Sir Charles said, reaching out and shaking her hand. "And this man, my dear, is the reason I dragged you all the way out here this morning. Annja Creed, Gianni Travino."

Bingo.

They shook hands.

"Good to meet you, Gianni."

Annja didn't miss the fact that he seemed to hold her hand a fraction of a moment longer than necessary.

They followed Charles inside.

"I suspect you're eager to get started so we'll save the tour for later and I'll take you to the room we've set up, if that's all right with you...?"

They made small talk as he led them through the house. She could feel Gianni's gaze on her as they walked, and she assumed he was sizing her up. Her long auburn hair, athletic form and decidedly feminine curves were likely a far cry from the stuffy museum heads he'd been dealing with about the library.

Then again, he might just be admiring her for totally different reasons. And wouldn't that be nice?

Yes, it would. She hadn't had a date in what felt like forever; she been too busy dashing here and there around the globe on behalf of *Chasing History's Monsters,* never mind her unofficial role as champion of the innocent.

Charles took them to a small room off the second floor. The diary was waiting for her in the center of the table like a long-lost friend and she went to it eagerly, pulling on the pair of white cotton gloves Charles gave her. Then he and Gianni excused themselves to go back to the meal they'd been sharing. Annja didn't want a thing. She was too excited.

The journal was thin, bound in dark leather and tied together with a red ribbon that had seen better days. Maybe that's why Charles Davies had tied his invitation with a ribbon. *Cute.* It rested on a glass platform designed so she could observe the specimen from all sides. It came equipped with two lamps, one shining down on the book from above and the other shining up on it from below. A legal pad and pencil lay on the table, in case she wanted to take notes.

Annja unzipped her knapsack, removing both her laptop and her digital camera. Booting the laptop, she connected it with a thin white cable to the camera and, after verifying the link between the two devices was working properly, began taking photos. This was so much a part of her standard procedure that it had become second nature to her. She always made a visual record of the artifact first, before beginning a more hands-on examination, and she had no intention of taking shortcuts now just because she wasn't in the field. What she was doing was simply good science, and if there was anything she prided herself on, it was being thorough. That way, the client couldn't ever accuse her of being sloppy or, worse yet, unprofessional. Her reputation was all she had in this line of work.

Finished with the camera, she turned her attention to the journal itself. She untied the ribbon and set it gently aside. With anticipation thrumming through her veins, she opened the book and stared at the crisp, clean handwriting on the first page. The Italian unfurled smoothly in her mind.

The morning began with a personal summons from the czar.

Three uninterrupted hours later she closed the journal and sat back. Charles and Gianni must have looked in on her, but she hadn't noticed them and fortunately they'd let her be. The legal pad beside her was covered with notes, and a fresh set of pictures, this time of some of the journal's pages, were displayed on the laptop. The journal was just what Gianni and, by extension, Charles had claimed it to be—a firsthand account of the design and construction of the vault commissioned by Ivan the Terrible to house the Library of Gold.

At first Fioravanti's excitement at being chosen for such an important project had practically leaped off the page and he'd been clear and direct in his language. This changed once he began to suspect that he might never live to see the finished result. By the last several pages he'd become downright evasive in his wording.

But what had interested Annja the most was the final page of the journal. Unlike all of the others, this one was clearly in code, with a series of letters laid out in a rectangular arrangement with eleven rows of eighteen letters.

```
CAECPARTIZSNAIIYOI
AETPCIOUIRCIEIEUTC
WRRWODTOAAEEINMOFN
NTWTBAURYTIOHUPSUO
SNROTWESUVTKUAIASR
AECTMTSIBUNRASHYAR
LDEREGOWOTSWONIUHT
TTCUDUSIHOOASISELE
RMNINEEEREUNNGPFYD
MNOGAPIOOADTSDETUL
IFEUEFGSENRSSTOETO
```

It was a form of substitution code and, luckily, one she was familiar with. The trick was to lay out the message with the proper number of rows, each with the right number of letters, until something made sense when you read down the vertical rows.

After a little bit of trial and error, Annja settled on twenty-two rows, each with nine letters.

```
CAECPARTI
ZSNAIIYOL
AETPCLOUL
RCIEIEUTC
WRRWODTOA
AEEINMOFN
NTWTBAURY
TIOHUPSUO
SNROTWESU
VTKUAIASR
AECTMTSIB
UNRASHYAR
LDEREGOWO
TSWONUUHT
TTCUDISIH
OOASISELE
RMNINEEER
EUNNGPFYD
MROGAPIOO
ADTSDETUL
IEEUEFGSF
NRSSTOETO
```

Then, reading down the rows moving from left to right, Annja spelled out the entire message, inserting breaks between words where they seemed most appropriate. To her surprise, it had been coded into English.

CZAR WANTS VAULT TO REMAIN A SECRET. INTENDS TO MURDER ENTIRE WORK CREW. CANNOT ESCAPE WITHOUT AROUSING SUSPICION BUT AM SENDING A DETAILED MAP WITH GIUSEPPE FOR YOU TO USE AS YOU SEE FIT. GET OUT WHILE YOU STILL CAN. YOUR BROTHER DOLFO.

If we could only get our hands on that map…

Charles's confident smile. Did he already have it? Is that why he's so convinced the journal will lead him to the library?

There was only one way to find out.

Annja took a photograph of the page containing the unbroken code and then one of the decoded message she'd worked out on her scratch pad. Afterward she packed everything up and emerged from the examination room to find Charles's butler, a tall, thin balding man with tufts of gray hair sprouting out of his ears and dressed in a sharply pressed black suit, waiting for her.

"Sir Charles and his guest have retired to the study. Sir Charles left instructions for me to guide you there, if that would be all right with you?"

Annja indicated the hallway before them with a sweep of her arm. "Lead on."

He took her down a few of the hallways she'd passed through earlier on her way to the examination room and then up a set of stairs to a room on the third floor. Gianni and Charles were deep in discussion over what looked to be a map—presumably of Moscow—but broke off when Annja arrived. The butler served them all drinks—Scotch for their host, espresso for Gianni and a mug of hot cocoa for Annja—and then they settled down to discuss their next steps. Annja and Gianni sat in leather armchairs in front of the desk with Charles in his wheelchair between them.

Annja didn't waste any time asking the question that was burning her up inside.

"Do you have it?"

Charles looked at her with a cautious expression. "Have what?"

"The map, of course. Or did you think a simple substitution code was going to trip me up?"

He laughed aloud, delighted, it seemed, with both her ability to figure out the code and her attitude. He turned to Gianni and said, "Decoding that message took us, what? Seventy-two hours?"

"Seventy-four and a half," the younger man replied, his gaze intent on her.

Annja pretended not to notice. "Since I obviously

passed your test with flying colors, let's get down to brass tacks. What exactly am I here for?"

"I should think that would be obvious by now," Charles replied. "I want you to lead an expedition to find the lost library."

Annja wasn't surprised. From the moment he'd mentioned the ancient library she knew that was where he was headed. But she also knew there was much more to an expedition than just deciding to conduct one.

"While I certainly appreciate the confidence you've shown in me..." she began, but got no further.

Davies held his hand up. "Now just hang on a minute," he told her. "Hear me out before you go telling me how crazy this is."

She hadn't been thinking quite that negatively, but waved to him to continue nonetheless.

"There have been more than eighteen well-funded attempts to find the library in the past fifty years, including two by Soviet leaders Joseph Stalin and Nikita Khrushchev. All of them have ultimately failed," Charles said. "I have no intention of having my expedition join that long and illustrious list.

"That's why I want to hire you, Annja. You have far more experience than any of the other expedition leaders I would be forced to consider if you turn me down. Though I'm confident you won't," he hastened to add.

Don't be so sure of that.

"Money is no object, so you will have the best gear and whatever equipment you need to retrieve the library once you have confirmed its location. I will also call on my contacts in Russia to provide you whatever access and assistance you need to be successful."

She had no doubt that his connections would be invaluable, as half the trouble on expeditions like this was securing the right to go where they wanted to go and search where they wanted to search. But she still wasn't confident about his motives.

"What is it you expect to do with the library once we find it?" she asked.

For just a moment Charles appeared startled, as if the thought had never occurred to him.

"Is that what you're concerned about? Rest easy, Miss Creed. If you locate—" he shook his head "—excuse me, *when* you locate it, the library will be turned over intact to the proper authorities inside the Russian government."

It was a reasonable response, but Annja found herself pushing him just a bit further. "Right after you pocket a hefty finder's fee, right?"

Charles laughed outright. "Look around you, Annja," he said, indicating with a sweep of his hands the house, the grounds, his entire business empire by extension, she supposed. "The media claims I have more money than God and you know what? That's probably the only time I've ever agreed with them.

I set a record last year for the most consecutive appearances on *Forbes* magazine's Top Ten Wealthiest People list. What on earth would I do with more money?"

It was the response she was looking for. The library was part of the world's cultural heritage, a glimpse into the beliefs and practices of the past. It belonged to the Russian people and shouldn't be locked away in some private collector's vault.

"Good," she said, "at least that's settled. But we're still faced with the issue of finding the map Fioravanti was talking about in his journal. You said you think you know where it is?"

Charles looked over at Gianni, who had been sitting patiently listening to their exchange. "Tell her," he said to the younger man.

Annja saw the flash of excitement in Gianni's eyes as he turned to face her. "According to what I've been able to discover, Ridolfo's brother gave the map to Kasmir Nabutov, their cousin by marriage and an Orthodox priest assigned to the Cathedral of the Annunciation. Everything I've found on the topic suggests that Nabutov secreted the map inside the *Gospel of Gold,* though how or exactly where I don't know."

She knew that Ivan the Terrible had gifted the *Gospel* to the cathedral in 1571, right about the same time the library had gone missing. Legend claimed the *Gospel* had once been a part of the library and that it contained a clue to the library's whereabouts, but it had been stored in the cathedral for hundreds of years with restricted access. Nobody had verified if the legend was true.

Given that they weren't getting in to see the *Gospel,* Annja didn't see how this was going to help them and said as much to the other two.

"As it turns out," Charles replied, "I have a colleague on the staff of the cathedral. I've made arrangements for the two of you to privately examine the *Gospel* the day after tomorrow."

The chance to see and touch the *Gospel of Gold* would have been enough to get her to agree to the trip. That she would be doing so as part of an expedition to find the lost library of Ivan the Terrible was icing on the cake.

Really good icing.

Now it was her turn to smile.

"So when do we get started?" she asked.

5

Gianni was waiting for her, two first-class Aeroflot tickets in his hand, when she arrived at the airport the next afternoon. The flight from JFK in New York to Moscow's Sheremetyevo International Airport was nine and a half hours, which would give them plenty of time to discuss how they intended to approach the *Gospel of Gold* and the ways Nabutov might have hidden information in its pages. First, however, Annja wanted to get to know her new companion better.

He, apparently, had the same idea.

"So," Gianni said as they settled into their seats, "what do you do when you're not traveling around the world searching for ancient artifacts and lost civilizations?"

"Oh, you know, the usual, I guess."

The usual? Ri-i-ight.

Somehow she didn't think protecting the innocent

while bearing a medieval mystical sword that was once carried by Joan of Arc fit into most people's definition of "the usual." It wasn't as if she could tell him the truth, and even if she did, he'd never believe it. Sometimes she almost didn't believe it herself.

The day she'd stumbled upon the last remaining fragment of Joan's shattered sword and, with her new friend Roux's help, brought it together with the other fragments he had spent hundreds of years collecting was etched indelibly in her mind. It had, quite literally, been a turning point, not just for her but for Roux and Garin Braden, as well. None of their lives had been the same since.

The sword had chosen her; she knew that now. It had reforged itself right before her very eyes and in doing so had selected her to be its next bearer. The role came with its own unique set of responsibilities, she'd discovered. Her own sense of justice seemed amplified when she carried the sword and several times she'd found herself unable to walk away from a situation as a result. Numbers and odds didn't matter, only that she acted to defend those who couldn't defend themselves when the opportunity presented itself.

Which seemed to be happening more and more frequently.

Annja didn't know how it all worked—at least, not yet. But she'd vowed that one day she would, because the mystery of it was like a constant irritation in the back of her logical, scientific brain.

Gianni, it seemed, wasn't going to settle for such a trite answer, though.

"Come on," he said, "you've got to give me more than that. Where'd you grow up?"

"New Orleans," she replied, intentionally not mentioning the orphanage she'd lived in or the nuns who'd been the only adult influences in her life throughout her childhood. He didn't need to know about that.

"What did you major in at school?"

"Bachelor's and master's degrees in archaeology, with a concentration in the medieval and Renaissance periods."

"And now you work for a cable television show. How do you like that?"

While it was an interesting question, it wasn't one that necessarily had an easy answer. She didn't particularly care for the show's sensationalism, but she appreciated that it allowed her to travel throughout the world investigating ancient civilizations and the legends surrounding them. It was a means to an end and right now one that came in very handy when she considered the sword's influence on her life.

She explained how she felt about the show as best she could, then said, "Enough with the twenty questions. What about you?"

"Me? Not much to tell, really. Born and raised

outside of Milan with my two brothers. One became a doctor, the other an architect. The pride of my parents' eyes."

"And you?"

He grinned. "A painter. Annoyed them even more than I thought it would."

Annja laughed, but it was more from a sense that it was the kind of response he was expecting. She'd worked hard and done what the nuns had expected of her so that she could get out of there at the earliest opportunity. Why anyone would intentionally choose a path that wasn't what they wanted to do just to annoy another person, especially their parents, was beyond her.

"What do you paint?"

Gianni shrugged. "This and that. Landscapes, mostly. A few portraits now and then." He studied her, a mischievous gleam in his eye. "You should let me paint you. You would look beautiful in the light of an Italian sunset."

An image flashed through Annja's mind, the two of them in a Tuscan farmhouse, the orange-red light of the setting sun streaming in through a nearby window, splashing across her supine form, warming her bare skin as Gianni looked on from a painter's stool a few feet away, close enough to reach out and touch...

Down, girl. It had been too long since she'd spent any time with the opposite sex.

Not wanting him to guess at her line of thought,

Annja assumed an indignant expression. "What's that supposed to mean?" she asked archly. "I need Italian sunlight to bring me up to your standards?"

For a moment, he just gaped at her. "Wait…that's not what I meant," he stammered, trying to recover. "I mean, of course you're beautiful, but the sunlight—"

Gianni sat and stared at her. "Very funny," he finally said. Their laughter served to bring them out of that awkward get-to-know-you stage and they spent the rest of the time before dinner chatting comfortably on topics ranging from the art of the Italian Renaissance to the Yankees' chance at another World Series. Once the flight attendant had cleared the dinner dishes, Annja decided to catch some sleep to help her adjust to the time change once they arrived in Moscow. Wrapping a blanket around her shoulders, she curled up with a pillow against the window and drifted off to sleep with the hum of the engines in her ears.

THE REST OF THE FLIGHT passed without difficulty and the pilot brought them in for a bumpy but otherwise uneventful landing just before midnight local time. Neither of them had checked their bags, so they were able to bypass baggage claim and reached the immigration processing area ahead of most of the other passengers. Annja handed their passports to a blonde woman in the blue uniform of the Federal Migration Service.

"What is the reason for your visit?" the officer asked, looking up at them as she compared their faces to their photos.

"Vacation."

It wasn't exactly true, but telling the officer that they were here to hunt for the long-lost library of Ivan the Terrible, one of Mother Russia's most feared despots, didn't seem the wisest move.

The officer scanned Annja's passport and then waited for her computer to process the information. Once it had, she picked up a rubber entry stamp and raised it over an open page of the passport only to hesitate at the last moment after glancing at what came up on her computer screen.

She lowered her hand without using the stamp.

Annja didn't like that, didn't like it at all.

A sense of unease slowly unfurled itself in her gut.

"You are together, yes?" the officer asked Annja, while inclining her head toward Gianni.

For a moment Annja thought the other woman was asking if the two of them were a couple. She opened her mouth to say no, but then realized what she was really being asked.

"That's right," she replied. "We are traveling to-gether." She smiled, hoping to get one in return.

She didn't.

The officer picked up Annja's passport a second

time and gave it closer scrutiny, which only increased Annja's growing unease.

"Is there a problem?" she asked.

The officer ignored her. She dialed a number on her phone, waited for it to be answered and then said a few short phrases in Russian, glancing only once at Annja in the process.

Annja knew a handful of languages, but unfortunately Russian wasn't one of them.

She desperately wanted to know what the officer was saying.

The officer hung up, got up from behind her desk and disappeared through a door in the back behind her station, all without saying a word to Annja or Gianni.

"What's going on?" he asked.

Annja just shook her head. "I'm not sure."

She glanced over the counter, trying to read whatever was on the officer's computer monitor, but it was angled too far to the left for her to get a clear look. She thought she could see the edge of a photo, a head shot perhaps, maybe even her own, but the reflection of the overhead lights on the screen kept her from being certain. Their passports were no longer on the counter, which could only mean the officer had taken them with her.

That wasn't a good sign.

"You're not an international fugitive by any chance, are you?"

She knew Gianni was joking, but the remark sent a shiver down her spine just the same. She'd had more than her fair share of police encounters since taking up the sword. More than once she'd had to employ creative storytelling when it came to explaining away the bodies she'd been forced to leave in her wake. She'd always acted in self-defense, but proper explanations would have required revealing the sword's existence and that was something she simply hadn't been prepared to do.

Had something she'd done in the past finally caught up with her?

6

The sound of a door closing caught her attention and Annja looked up to see the blond officer walking back toward her, with two other immigration agents in tow. Both were large men, with wide shoulders and several inches on Annja. If they weren't imposing enough, the sight of the handguns holstered on their belts clearly indicated they meant business.

The blonde opened the low gate separating the passengers from the immigration officials and waved Annja and Gianni through.

"This way."

It was voiced as a request, but Annja knew they had little choice. Something must have set off a red flag somewhere, leaving them with the option of either following orders or trying to make a break for it. Neither course of action was all that appealing.

Her instincts were screaming at her to get out of there, but to reach the street, they would have to get past not only the immigration officers but also the customs officials at their stations farther down the corridor, and both groups were armed.

The immigration officers formed up around them and marched them off down the hall to curious stares from their former fellow passengers. They were led to a small windowless room that contained a table and four chairs, two on either side. Annja had seen her share of interrogation rooms. She glanced around, trying to spot the security cameras, to no avail. She knew they were there, somewhere, and had no doubt that the room was also bugged. She hoped Gianni was smart enough to figure it out for himself, because there was no way of warning him without giving away that they had something to hide.

Just going to have to play it by ear and hope for the best.

Their guide asked them to take a seat, said something about getting them water and closed the door behind her on the way out.

Annja didn't even try the knob; she knew it would be locked.

Not that a locked door would have stopped her. She could have called her sword to her at any moment and made short work of both the lock and the door. But that wouldn't get them to the bottom of what was happening and would only serve to cement their guilt in the minds of their captors.

They could always use the sword to free themselves if it proved necessary later.

They sat there, staring at the four walls, for what felt like hours. Twice Gianni tried to engage her in conversation, to get her to discuss their situation and why she thought they might be in here, but she shushed him both times.

She didn't want to give them any more ammunition than they already had. Whatever that might be.

Ten minutes passed, then fifteen, before the door opened and the biggest man Annja had ever seen stepped inside the room. She and Gianni immediately got to their feet. He was so tall that he had to duck to get through the doorway and his wide shoulders filled his jacket near to bursting. His sheer presence was intimidating, never mind his scowling expression. Annja found herself subconsciously shifting her feet into a wider defensive stance, preparing for a confrontation. She needn't have worried, though, for the man's bulldog face split into an equally wide grin when he caught sight of her.

"Rasputin's ghost!" he exclaimed. "It *is* you."

The man's reaction was so unexpected that Annja could only stand there and stare.

The newcomer crossed the room, one enormous paw extended, and took Annja's hand in his own and shook.

"Welcome. Welcome to Moscow. I am Yuri Basilovich and, I assure you, I am your biggest fan in all of Russia."

"Fan?" Annja asked, still trying to make sense of what was happening.

"Yes. Yes, of course! I have seen all of your episodes at least twice, sometimes more. If there is anything you need, anything at all, you let me know, *da?*"

Annja blinked and finally understood that she was standing in a Russian interrogation room talking to this giant of a man because he was a fan of her show. All the tension and anxiety slipped from her system in a rush, leaving her light-headed. When she found her voice, she said, "I'm very pleased to meet you, Yuri, but I must admit to being confused. My colleague and I have been held here as if we were criminals. Would it have not been easier if you'd simply said hello to us when we were in the immigration line?"

The big man's expression went from enthusiasm to abject horror. He turned to the immigration officer behind him, one of the men who had escorted them here in the first place, and fired off a rapid stream of Russian. Annja didn't speak the language, but judging from his tone, Yuri wasn't happy. He must not have appreciated the answer he received, either, for it elicited another blast from him.

After dressing down his subordinate, Yuri turned back to face Annja.

"I must beg your forgiveness, Miss Creed," he said, the embarrassment plain on his face. "I had not wanted to miss a chance to meet you in the unlikely event that you came through our facility, so I had placed an alert in the system keyed to your name. When my subordinates saw that, they wrongly assumed you had done something illegal and detained you. Unfortunately, I was not on the premises at the time."

Annja was flattered but also annoyed. To think that a man would go to so much trouble on the slim chance that she might one day come through his airport was one thing, but being kept locked in a small room for more than an hour was something else entirely. It was not an auspicious beginning to their trip.

We've wasted enough time, she thought. We need to get out of here and back on schedule.

Annja smiled at the big Russian. "I understand completely, Yuri. I'm always happy to meet a fan of *Chasing History's Monsters* and so I say we chalk this up to an unfortunate miscommunication and leave it at that. What do you say?"

Yuri's head bobbed up and down. "I couldn't agree more, Miss Creed. And if I may, perhaps you'll let me provide an escort to your hotel to make up for the time that you have lost?"

"That's not necessary, Yuri...."

"No, I insist," he replied, and wouldn't take no for an answer.

Under Yuri's direction they were hustled through the airport and out through a special VIP door away from the general traffic. A black Mercedes limousine pulled into view just as they came out of the building.

"Where are you staying?" Yuri asked.

"The Marriott Grand Hotel on Tverskaya Street."

"Of course."

Yuri placed their roller bags in the trunk, opened the door of the Mercedes, waiting for Gianni and Annja to climb into the backseat before saying a few words to the driver. Turning back to Annja, he handed her his card. "The driver will take you directly to your hotel, Miss Creed, and the fare is taken care of, courtesy of the Federal Migration Service. If there is anything else I can do to make your stay more comfortable, you need only call."

Annja thanked him and, as the driver pulled away from the curb, slipped Yuri's card into her pocket.

You never knew when having a friend in the Russian immigration service could come in handy.

7

The hotel was located on legendary Tverskaya Street in the heart of Moscow, within walking distance of Red Square. The driver took them there without delay and with a minimum of fuss. Upon checking in, they discovered that Sir Charles had reserved two adjoining executive-level rooms for them on the ninth floor, away from the hotel traffic.

The rooms were well appointed and spacious. From Annja's window she could see the colorful spires of Saint Basil's Cathedral and the long wall of the Kremlin itself. They wouldn't have any trouble getting there in the morning. Annja quickly stowed the one bag she'd brought with her and then knocked on the door connecting her room to Gianni's.

"It's open," he called.

Annja stepped inside to find him staring out the window at the Kremlin a few blocks away.

"I never thought I'd get this far," he said wistfully,

without taking his eyes off what was perhaps Russia's most iconic building. Annja knew just how he felt. She'd been there herself, more times than she could count, when all the hard work had come together and she stood before the object of her search, wondering just how it was all going to turn out. She knew the mix of eagerness and doubt he had to be feeling because she was experiencing it, too. Tomorrow was going to be an important day for both of them.

"Shall we give Charles a call and let him know we've arrived?" she asked.

Gianni handed over the satellite phone Charles had given them. Annja made sure the speakerphone was activated and then placed the call.

"Any difficulties?" Charles asked, after they had exchanged pleasantries.

"No, no trouble here," Annja told him, deciding that the encounter with her "number-one fan" was something he didn't need to hear about for the time being.

"Good. Glad to hear that nonsense at the airport didn't amount to anything."

Gianni, clearly amused, glanced in her direction.

Their employer was well connected, indeed, if he'd heard about that already, she thought. Have to remember that in the future.

His point made, Charles went on. "I've arranged for you to meet an old colleague of mind, Semyon

Petrescu, at the Cathedral of the Annunciation tomorrow afternoon. He is the curator of the rare book collection housed there and he has graciously agreed to give you a few hours to examine the *Gospel of Gold*. He thinks you're doing research for a thesis, so let's keep him in the dark about our true purpose, all right?"

"Thesis. Got it." She had no idea what kind of thesis she was supposed to be writing, but she was sure she'd figure something out when the time came. Charles went on, providing the details of where and when they were to meet his colleague, which Gianni jotted down on the notepad next to the phone. After instructing them to call in tomorrow after visiting the cathedral, their employer bid them goodbye and disconnected the call.

Back in her room, Annja washed up, changed into her pajamas and climbed into bed. Despite the couple of hours' sleep she'd grabbed aboard the plane, she was asleep moments after her head hit the pillow.

THE NEXT DAY ANNJA was up with the sunrise, the effect of the long flight lost in her enthusiasm for the search to come. She pulled on a T-shirt and sweats, pushed the coffee table and chair back against the wall to clear some space in the middle of the room and then reached into the otherwhere for her sword.

The broadsword slid smoothly into existence, appearing with the speed of thought, the hilt fitting her palm as if it was specially made for her and her alone. The weapon was finely balanced and in the time she'd carried it she'd become very skilled with it. That didn't stop her from practicing, which was just what she intended to do now.

She spent the next forty-five minutes working through a variety of sword katas, stylized sequences of moves designed to mimic the attack and defense response of an actual sword fight. The physical practice allowed the motions to settle into her muscle memory so that they would be there at her beck and call when she needed them.

After her workout, she called down to room service and had them deliver a breakfast of bacon and eggs, which she ate with relish. Then she showered, dressed and was at her laptop doing additional background research on the cathedral when Gianni knocked on her door.

They left the hotel and walked down the street toward the Kremlin. From her morning's research, Annja knew that the Cathedral of the Annunciation had been built by Ivan the Terrible's grandfather, Grand Duke Ivan III, as part of his general expansion of the Kremlin. It was smaller than the other two grand cathedrals that were nearby, but from the time of Ivan the Terrible's coronation as czar of Russia, the royal family had worshipped, gotten married and baptized their children inside the walls of this cathedral. Even after the capital had been moved to

Saint Petersburg, the cathedral had continued to play an important role in the lives of the royal family.

It was a fitting place to begin their search for the library.

The official entrance to the Kremlin was through the Savior's Gate, located in the base of the gothic-turreted Spasskaya Tower. A small crowd of tourists were gathered outside, taking pictures of the clock hanging high above on the tower's face, and Annja and Gianni were forced to thread their way through them to reach the entrance where a guard was checking IDs.

Annja noted several people crossing themselves and doffing their hats as they passed through the gates and she was reminded of how the tower was reputed to be possessed with miraculous powers and would supposedly protect the Kremlin from enemy invasion. Horses passing through its gates were said to shy in fear, and legend had it that Napoleon's own horse had reared in fright when he'd tried to enter without showing his respect.

They handed their passports to the guard when it was their turn and told him they had an appointment to see Dr. Petrescu. The guard gave them visitor badges and let them through.

The cathedral was located on the southwest corner of Cathedral Square, where it was directly connected to the main building of the Grand Kremlin Palace complex. Its nine golden domes shone in the morning sun as they approached, their glow reflecting off the white limestone facades beneath. They entered through the doors decorated with gold foil at the top of the south staircase as they'd been instructed, Annja cataloging the fact that it was this staircase, rather than the eastern one, that had been added by Ivan the Terrible in 1570.

Another guard sat behind a desk just inside the doors and they repeated their goal to him. He picked up the phone, made a quick call and then asked them to wait. A few minutes later a man came down the hall toward them, dressed in a dark suit and tie. Given the lines on his face and his thinning gray hair, Annja guessed he was in his early sixties. He smiled as he saw them and when he got closer extended his hand.

"I am Semyon Petrescu and, unless my instincts are off, you must be Ms. Creed and Mr. Travino."

They shook hands.

"Sir Charles tells me you're interested in taking a look at the *Gospel of Gold,* is that right?" Semyon asked as he ushered them past the guard and headed back down the hall in the direction he'd come.

"It is," Annja replied, stepping in beside their host and letting Gianni bring up the rear. "I'm gathering data for a thesis on the decorative art and illuminated manuscripts of sixteenth-century religious texts, a study that wouldn't be complete without a section on the *Gospel of Gold.*"

Annja was confident her knowledge of the subject would be enough to provide a convincing cover for them and hoped all the while that Semyon wouldn't ask Gianni any questions. Thankfully he didn't, and by the time they reached the room where they were to examine the almost five-hundred-year-old manuscript, Annja and Semyon were chatting like old friends.

The examination room was typical of those she'd used at other facilities, just a small square room with a table in the center and decent lighting overhead. A metal case rested on the tabletop, two pairs of white cotton gloves lying beside it. A surveillance camera hung from the ceiling in one corner.

Their host led them over to the table and then went around to the opposite side. He took his own pair of white gloves out of his pocket and pulled them on, indicating with a nod that they should do the same.

"A few reminders," he said as he turned the case toward him and punched the combination into the keypad lock set in the top. "Gloves must be worn at all times and photography of any kind, with or without flash, is strictly prohibited. Written transcripts of the entire volume are available, complete with reproductions of the artwork, and I can have one of these made available to you should you need it."

He said something else after that, but Annja didn't hear it, her attention riveted on the gold-and-jewel-encrusted tome he lifted out of the specimen case and set on the table in front of them.

The *Gospel of Gold.*

It was an oversize book, long and wide like an accountant's ledger, and several inches thick. The cover was filigree gold, inset with uncut precious gems—topazes, tourmalines and sapphires from the looks of them. It drew her forward like a moth to a flame.

"Amazing, isn't it?" Semyon asked.

It certainly was.

8

Up close, Annja could see five circular enamels set in the cover, one on each corner and a larger one in the center. All five were surrounded by wreathed inscriptions linked to one another in nielloed gold. The image in the center was that of the risen Christ, while those in the corners represented various saints praying or studying.

It was a stunning piece of workmanship, made all the more so by the knowledge that the work had been done by hand in the sixteenth century.

"My office is just down the hall," Semyon said, "so if you need anything, dial 475."

He pointed to an old-fashioned push-button phone hanging on the wall in the corner. He didn't mention the state-of-the-art security camera that hung from the ceiling above it. It was positioned so that most of the room would be visible, but Annja doubted the feed would be monitored 24/7.

Then again, this was Russia....

Satisfied that all was in order, their host left them to it.

Annja and Gianni spent the next several hours going through the *Gospel* one page at a time, carefully examining each one before moving on to the next. As they had decided the night before, Annja concentrated on the text of each page while Gianni focused on the artwork that decorated the borders and surrounded the drop cap that started each section of text. If Gianni's research was correct, somewhere in the *Gospel*'s gilded pages were instructions to find the map that would lead them to the library.

The workmanship was beautiful. The scribe had used bold clean strokes and the words and images seemed to jump right off the page at her. It was hard to believe this was a book that had been produced more than four hundred years ago.

Beauty aside, however, after hours of careful observation they could find nothing that pointed to the location or even the existence of the map that Fioravanti had mentioned in his journal. They'd been through the complete text and, having arrived at the blank page at the end, Annja was ready to admit they might need to rethink their approach.

She was used to setbacks and suggested they take a break, come at it again later with fresh eyes.

"Damn it!" Gianni swore, getting up from the

table and pacing in frustration. "We can't give up now. It's here somewhere, I *know* it is!"

"No one is giving up," she said soothingly, glancing over his shoulder at the camera on the other side of the room, hoping he'd recognize the unspoken warning in her eyes. She didn't want to offer their hosts any excuse for removing them from the room. "I'm just suggesting we take a short break that's all."

With her gaze still on her companion, Annja reached out to close the book and in the process her fingers brushed across the surface of the end page.

Something tugged at the cotton glove covering the tip of one finger.

One-one-hundredth of a degree less pressure and she never would have felt it.

She looked down at the page in front of her but didn't see anything that was immediately obvious and a second pass with her gloved finger across its surface didn't turn up whatever it was that had snagged it in the first place, either.

But something was there.

She was certain of it.

A tingling sense of anticipation built in her gut, the one that she usually experienced just before a big find. And that told her she was on to something here.

It occurred to her that the glove might be the problem, that the thickness of the cotton was keeping her from feeling whatever was on the page.

She didn't want to be caught on camera violating the rules they'd agreed to abide by.

Gianni had stopped on the far side of the table from her, his body positioned almost directly in front of the camera.

She slid the book closer to his end of the table, then moved around to his side and gave him what she hoped would appear to any observer like a friendly, one-armed hug. Supporting a stressed-out colleague.

As she leaned in close to him, she whispered, "Block the camera with your body. I found something."

His eyes widened, but he did as she asked.

With her hands in front of her and both of their bodies between the book and the camera, Annja pulled her glove off and ran the tips of her fingers across the empty page.

Now she could feel it, a series of raised bumps, as if someone had pushed down on the other side of the page with a pointed object. Not hard enough to be seen with the naked eye.

You'd have to know it was there in order to find it.

She closed her eyes and concentrated on what she was feeling.

Three numbers.

2-6-8.

That was all.

Concerned that the *Gospel of Gold* had been out of closed-circuit view for too long, Annja pulled her glove back on and stepped away from the table, revealing to the camera that the book was in the same place it had been a moment before.

Gianni was practically shaking with his need to know what she had found so he dropped his voice and she quickly filled him in.

"Three numbers?" he said. "That's it?"

"That's it."

He swore in Italian, and even if she hadn't understood every word he said, she still would have been able to get the gist of it.

"What's the problem now?" she asked.

"It's another bloody code, isn't it?"

It more than likely *was* a code. It wasn't a set of compass directions or GPS coordinates; there weren't enough numerals for the first and it would be a few hundred years after the book was manufactured before GPS would be anyone's idea.

Gianni might not like codes, but Annja did. Codes, puzzle boxes, riddles—she loved them all. Fioravanti had used a substitution code, so it made sense that his colleague would do the same. And if that were the case, then each number stood for something specific.

But what?

She looked down at the numbers again.

2-6-8.

Certain things stood out immediately. All the numbers were not only even, but they were also divisible by two. And when you added the first two together, you got the third.

But what do the numbers represent?

She glanced at Gianni to see him flipping through the pages at the beginning of the *Gospel,* clearly looking for something specific.

"What is it?" she asked.

"Not sure yet," he replied. He found the page he was looking for and began running his finger down the text, counting to himself as he went. "Hang on..."

But a moment later he leaned back away from the book in frustration. "It's nothing. Never mind."

But Annja was getting that feeling again and she wasn't ready to let the puzzle go quite yet.

"I want to hear it."

Gianni sighed. "I thought the numbers might stand for specific words in the text. The first number would represent the word, the second the line on which it is found and the third the page number. So 2-6-8 would be the second word on the sixth line of the eighth page of the text."

Annja could feel her pulse pick up as she realized he might be on to something. "That's good, Gianni. Really good!" She turned the book toward her.

"Well, the word *the* is going to get us really far."

Annja stopped to think it through. Gianni was right; one word wasn't going to get them very far. But what if the means to find the next word was wrapped up in the instructions for the first?

In the first clue, the first two numbers, 2 and 6, combined to equal the third, 8. What if she stuck with that pattern? she thought. Combined the second and third numbers to get the fourth, the third and fourth to get the fifth, and so on?

She pulled the book closer and tried it out. The first five combinations gave her the words *the, Judah, Yaweh, dawn* and *worship*. Not exactly the kind of revelation she was looking for. And she couldn't continue with the process, because the next combination would result in a line number that was greater than the lines on any given page.

"What did I tell you? Useless," Gianni said, after watching her work for a moment.

Annja wasn't yet ready to give up.

What if she divided each number in the combination by the number of the "clue" she was currently trying to solve? The number set of 2-6-8 would stay the same, since it was the first clue and therefore would be divided by one. But 6-8-14 would become 3-4-7 when it was divided by two and 8-14-22 would become 3-5-8 if she rounded up to the next nearest divisible number.

Using this system, the first three combinations gave them three words.

The key to...

"Keep going," Gianni whispered urgently.

She kept at it until she ran out of numbers that would fit into the makeshift equation given the limitations of the lines on the page and the number of pages in the text. When she was done, she arranged the words she'd jotted down into lines that seemed to make sense.

The key to Grozny's treasure
Lies in the hand of the Lady
Who stands in the center
Of the rising flames.

Goose bumps rose along Annja's arms as she stared at the words in front of her.

The Lady who stands in the center of the rising flames...

Given her own personal history with a particular woman who had done just that, Annja was momentarily at a loss. Gianni must have noticed something was wrong. He reached out and put a hand on her lower arm.

"Are you all right?" he asked.

She nodded, then shook herself.

Just a coincidence.

Coincidence, or a sign that she was on the right path.

"Grozny. That's Russian for *fearsome,* right?" Gianni asked, studying the four lines as if the meaning of life itself could be found in their depths.

Annja nodded. "*Fearsome* or *terrible* usually, yeah."

"So it's clearly referencing Ivan the Terrible."

The coded message was the first actual evidence they had that Gianni's research had been right. That his ancestor Fioravanti had entrusted the information about the map to his relative, Nabutov.

"That's how I would read it."

"What about the next part, then? Who is the Lady? And what are the flames she is standing in? That doesn't make a lot of sense…."

But it did to Annja, thanks to all the research she had done about the Kremlin and its surroundings. Never mind a few choice memories from having been raised in a Catholic orphanage.

She pointed to the word *Lady* at the end of the second line. "The Lady is the Most Holy Lady Theotokos, otherwise known as the Virgin Mary. To Russian Orthodox believers, as with Catholics, she is venerated, a very important figure."

Gianni nodded. "Right. The main chapel of Saint Basil's Cathedral right here in Red Square is dedicated to her."

"And it's also the center referred to in the third line."

"How do you know that?"

"Because the cathedral stands in the geometric center of the Garden Ring, the circular avenue that runs around the heart of Moscow on the very spot where the first protective rampart and wall were built by Feodor I back in 1591."

"And the flames…?"

"Legend has it that the cathedral was designed to resemble a bonfire burning into the Russian night."

A grin spread across Gianni's face. "So the map is hidden in the statue of the Virgin Mary—"

"—which stands in the middle of Saint Basil's Cathedral a few hundred yards away from here," Annja finished for him.

9

In the wake of their discovery, Annja called down to Dr. Petrescu's office and let him know they had finished with the *Gospel of Gold*. It seemed to take forever for him to arrive in the examination room and even longer for him to pack the *Gospel* back into its protective case. Annja kept up a running commentary on the impressiveness of the *Gospel*'s illuminations and how they compared to other books of the same time period. When Petrescu finally had the *Gospel* secured in its carrying case, he led them back to the security desk where she thanked him and they said their goodbyes.

Once outside Annja had to restrain Gianni from rushing across the square to Saint Basil's. It was midafternoon and the square was filled with hundreds of people, most of them tourists. She felt the same urge to see if the map remained where it had been secreted all those years ago, but a couple of foreigners rushing across Red Square as if their lives were in danger would certainly capture the attention of the authorities. Particularly in this age of suicide bombers and terrorist attacks. The last thing they needed was to be dragged into another windowless room for a round of aggressive questioning.

"Slow down," she told him. "We need to think about this."

"What's to think about?" Gianni asked impatiently. "We find the statue, grab the map and get out of there."

"In front of all these people?" She waved her hand at the crowds around them. "I don't think so."

"Well, what do you suggest, then?"

"There's no sense blindly rushing into this," she told him. "The map has been there for several hundred years. Another hour or two won't make a difference. Let's go inside, take a look around and work out a plan."

Reluctantly he conceded the point and they began to thread their way through the crowd, headed for the colorful domes of Saint Basil's. Impulsively Annja slipped her arm through Gianni's and received a wide smile in return. The day was warm and clear and Annja was suddenly feeling very good about the work they'd accomplished so far.

Saint Basil's Cathedral's real name, she knew, was the Cathedral of the Protection of Most Holy Theotokos on the Moat, which made her thankful for its more common nickname. Its proper name came from the alleged appearance of the apparition of the Virgin above the city of Constantinople when it was being threatened by a large Slavic fleet. Ivan had ordered the cathedral built in 1555 to commemorate the capture of Kazan and Astrakhan, which marked the final battle of the Russo-Kazan wars. The original building had consisted of eight smaller, side churches surrounding a ninth, central one. A tenth was added thirty years later over the grave of a local saint and that's where its popular name had come from. The church's design was unlike any other building in Russia and the many-colored hues and pigments that decorated its exterior caused it to stand out in Red Square.

There was a line waiting to go in and the two of them joined it, doing their best to look like any other pair of tourists. As they moved inside, Annja was surprised by how narrow it was. Each chapel was smaller than she expected and the oddly turning corridors that connected them made it hard to see from one into the next. They pushed through the earlier chapels, until they reached the main one in the center.

The statue of the Virgin Mother stood on a raised platform set by itself inside a niche in the wall at the back of the room. Around it were more of the iconographic paintings, like those that decorated the rest of the cathedral's interior. The statue appeared to have been carved from a single piece of white marble and the artist had depicted her in her usual cloak and veil, with one arm above her head and her face raised lovingly toward heaven. The statue was surrounded by a marble railing that reached midthigh, allowing tourists to see the Holy Mother clearly but prevented them from touching her.

Annja stood at the edge of the rail, trying to get a better look at the statue's hands, but it was too far away to see the kind of detail she was looking for. She glanced around and then approached a middle-age tourist who was standing admiring the statue, as well. A digital camera with a long telephoto lens hung around about his neck.

"Excuse me, sir?"

He turned to her. *"Oui?"*

She switched to French. "I'm sorry to bother you, but I'm trying to get a closer look at the features of the Holy Mother's face. Would you mind if I used your camera?"

A smile had spread across his face at the sound of his mother tongue. "Of course," he replied, "my pleasure."

They moved back over to the railing, where he handed her the camera and showed her how to focus it. She didn't need the instruction, but suffered through it quietly. When he was finished, she brought the camera to her eye and focused in on the statue's left hand, the one hanging by Mary's side.

Even with the aid of the telephoto lens Annja couldn't see anything out of the ordinary. The hand, and the arm it was attached to, both seemed to be made from the same piece of marble as the rest of the statue. The same held true for the other hand, the one raised toward the ceiling.

If it had been easy to find, someone would have discovered it years ago.

She handed the camera back to the Frenchman, thanked him and then let Gianni know what she'd discovered.

"So now what?" he asked, eyeing the statue the way an addict might his latest fix.

"I'm not sure."

Moments later, the two of them found themselves alone in the small chapel. Despite all the time she'd spent cautioning her companion against rushing in and calling attention to themselves, Annja was gripped by a sudden sense of urgency. Before she knew it she found herself climbing over the railing surrounding the statue.

"Watch the door," she whispered to Gianni as he stared in astonishment at what she was doing. Her words had the desired effect, breaking him out of his surprise and sending him hustling across the room.

This is a bad idea, she told herself but didn't stop as she clambered up on the pedestal.

Her body blocked some of the light, sending shadows into the niche in which the statue stood, and so she pulled out her BlackBerry and used the flash-light app.

It was immediately clear that the statue had been carved from one large block of stone. The right hand flowed onto the lower arm and no matter what she did to it—pushed, pulled, tugged, twisted—she couldn't get it to move.

Very conscious of the seconds ticking away, Annja turned her attention to the left hand, the one that was raised over the statue's head.

It was still too high above the floor for her.

Cursing under her breath, she climbed onto the base of the platform, using the statue to steady herself. If anyone came in now they were in deep trouble.

She reached up, grabbed hold of the statue's right hand and began to apply some pressure.

To her surprise, the hand moved slightly.

"Got something," she whispered across the emptiness of the chapel without taking her eyes off what she was doing.

"Better hurry up," Gianni called in a stage whisper. "There's a group of tourists getting closer."

Annja pushed and pulled at the hand, her heart pounding.

It refused to move.

"You stupid son of a…" she muttered beneath her breath.

"They're getting closer!" Gianni called.

It was time for something drastic.

Holding her right arm out away from the statue, she reached into the otherwhere and drew forth her sword. Without hesitation she reached up and whacked the statue's hand once sharply with the flat of the blade.

The sound of the blade striking the stone rang out through the space around her, but by the time Gianni figured out where the sound was coming from and looked in her direction, the sword was gone. She'd released it back into the otherwhere.

This time, when she grabbed the statue's hand, it came free so suddenly that she nearly dropped it on the floor.

She immediately saw that it wasn't a solid piece of marble at all, but a hollowed-out shell.

Something was stuffed inside it.

"Annja!" This time there was no mistaking the panic in Gianni's voice.

She turned and leaped from the base of the statue to the top of the railing and had just stepped down onto the floor of the chapel when tourists came into the room, chatting noisily in a variety of languages. One of them glanced sharply in her direction and for a moment she thought the young man might have seen her up on the railing, but then he shook his head and looked away. No doubt he'd convinced himself it was absurd to even think someone had been where they were not supposed to be.

Annja turned her back on the group and shoved two fingers into the opening in the base of the hand, trying to fish out whatever was inside there. The tips of her fingers brushed against it, but on the third try she managed to snag it and slowly pull it out.

They had found the map.

10

Colonel Viktor Goshenko stared out the window of his office at Red Square and considered how little things had changed in his country since the rise of Gorbachev and his ridiculous notions of glasnost and perestroika. The names were different— prime minister rather than secretary general, the Federal Security Service instead of the Soviet Committee of State Security, otherwise known as the KGB— but not much else. The rich were still rich, the poor were still poor, and those without power craved it while those who had it used it mercilessly toward their own ends.

Goshenko was very happy to be one of the latter.

The intercom on his desk buzzed.

He stepped over to it and pressed the button with his thick finger. "Yes, Pavel?"

"There is a Semyon Pyotr on line one for you, Colonel."

For a moment, the name meant nothing to him. He stood there, frowning, his finger on the intercom. He was about to tell Pavel to get rid of whoever it was, when he finally made the connection.

Simon Peter. The first of the Apostles.

Of course.

The fool was trying to use code, to disguise his real identity. Except he was using his own first name in the process.

Idiot.

He picked up the phone.

"What do you have for me?" he asked, not bothering with introductions.

The caller, unfazed by Goshenko's rudeness, said, "A man and a woman were granted access to the archives today. They spent the majority of their time examining the *Gospel of Gold,* though for what I do not know. They kept their voices low and were guarded in what they said, but at one point the man grew excited and made a reference to the library."

There was only one library this particular informant could be referring to, and Goshenko felt his heart rate increase. He'd dreamed of the library only two nights ago and had awoken filled with a sense that his long quest was coming to an end. That soon the library and the riches it contained would be within his grasp.

And now this.

It seemed almost too good to be true.

"Did you recognize them?" Goshenko asked.

"Not the man, no. The woman, though, was familiar. She is the host of an American television show about ancient artifacts and legends. Her name is Annja Creed."

Goshenko reached for a pad of paper lying on his desktop, intending to make a note of the woman's name, but then thought better of it. The paranoia that had kept him alive through the purges of the past several years controlled his actions. He could remember the name easily enough; why create a paper trail that someone else could follow?

"Photos?"

"Yes, though they are not the best quality, as they were taken with a cell phone. Still, they should serve their purpose."

They would, indeed.

"Email them to this account immediately." Goshenko rattled off the address of a throwaway account he'd created, one of many, for just such a purpose.

There was a moment of silence on the other end of the line and then the caller came back on. "Done. I have also included the name and address of their hotel."

Goshenko frowned. "You followed them?"

"No, no, of course not," the other man said quickly, responding to the iciness that had slipped into Goshenko's tone. "They requested that translations of the *Gospel* be sent over to them at their hotel."

"That's good," Goshenko said, mollified. "After such excellent work, it would have been a shame to kill you."

He hung up before the other man could say anything else. Fear was always a good motivator and Goshenko never missed an opportunity to make use of it, to remind those beneath him of their respective positions. But even he had to admit the informant had made excellent use of an opportunity.

He turned to stare out the window at the tourists in Red Square. He wasn't seeing the weather, however, but rather the ancient scrolls and texts of Ivan the Terrible's long-lost library laid out before him. Proof that his decades-long search had not been in vain. With a sense of victory humming through his body, he considered his next move.

He needed to know more about this Creed woman.

He returned to his desk, woke up his computer and scoured the databases for any mention of her.

What he saw both encouraged and concerned him.

She appeared to be quite gifted in locating historic artifacts and puzzling the truth out of legends, if the consumer media was to be believed. Her list of accomplishments, particularly in the past few years, seemed as long as his arm. Time and again she had succeeded where others had failed, locating ancient cities and lost civilizations.

It was her very success rate that set Goshenko's thoughts whirring inside his head. His first inclination was to send a team to snatch her off the street. He had no doubt she'd break under questioning and tell him everything she knew about the library and its whereabouts because, in time, everyone broke.

But perhaps there was a better way....

He picked up his phone and dialed a number. "Send Sergeant Danislov to my office," he said, and then hung up

He turned and stared out the window once more, not seeing anything beyond the glass, his thoughts on the Creed woman as he waited for his subordinate to arrive.

It didn't take long.

Goshenko was always on the lookout for men with a particular set of talents, and Sergeant Danislov had come to his attention several years before after he'd been involved in a series of raids against terror cells in the highlands of Afghanistan. The raids had achieved their objectives, but had been sullied by rumors that the sergeant in charge, one Arkady Danislov, had gone above and beyond the rules of engagement.

In other words, he'd done what needed to be done and to hell with the morality of the situation.

Goshenko had needed a man like that on his staff to personally handle sensitive situations Goshenko didn't want on the books. It hadn't taken much to convince the sergeant that his future might be brighter under Goshenko's patronage. The colonel had arranged an interdepartmental transfer for Danislov and the man had been a permanent member of his staff ever since.

Danislov slipped into the room; he could move quietly for a man his size. Unlike most of the agents of the Federal Security Service he wasn't clean-shaven, but his goatee was neatly trimmed and his hair was cut short enough to satisfy even the most stringent military regulations. He wore civilian clothing and a pair of hiking boots, but there was no mistaking the past position he had held in the ramrod-erect way he carried himself. He came to a stop exactly ten inches in front of Goshenko's desk.

"You wanted to see me, sir?"

Goshenko waved him forward. "Thank you for coming, Sergeant. Two Americans visited the Cathedral of the Annunciation today as part of an unauthorized expedition to find the Library of Gold."

Danislov's eyebrow rose slightly, causing the scar on that side of his face to undulate for a moment, but that was his only reaction to the news.

Goshenko went on. "I want you to determine what it was they looked at and what they might have found as a result of their research. View the security tapes, talk to the curator—whatever is necessary—you understand?"

"Yes, sir."

"Good. The man you want to see over there is Semyon Petrescu. He shouldn't give you any trouble. Call me when you know something."

"Yes, sir."

Danislov resisted the urge to salute, a habit Goshenko knew he was trying hard to break, and headed out to follow his orders. Goshenko returned to his vigil.

This time, however, his gaze was drawn across the square to the gold-domed towers of the Annunciation Cathedral and he found himself wondering just what it was that the Americans had found there.

11

It didn't take long for Sergeant Danislov to get to the bottom of what the Americans had been looking for. He knew only one way of attacking a problem and that was head-on, so he took the obvious route to achieve his objectives. He visited Petrescu's office, questioned him over what was said while the Americans were examining the *Gospel of Gold* and then confiscated the surveillance video for the time in question.

Returning to his office in the Kremlin, he examined the material in preparation for briefing Colonel Goshenko.

Three hours later, he stood before the colonel's desk once more, laying out what he had discovered.

"Creed and her companion arrived midmorning and remained inside the Annunciation Cathedral until well after lunch. They were escorted to the examination room by Dr. Petrescu and the video footage shows that they never left the area until the doctor returned to escort them back outside. The only item they examined was the *Gospel of Gold*."

"Besides mentioning the library, did they indicate how they expected the *Gospel* to help them find it?" Goshenko asked.

A quick shake of Danislov's head. "Except for the man's one reference to the library, there is nothing clear on the audio recordings. They must have known they were being recorded. And had cause not to be."

Goshenko frowned at that. Danislov went on.

"According to Petrescu, the Americans were there to conduct research for a graduate thesis on illuminated manuscripts, but that is counter to the information he passed on to you about the library. Nor can I find any information that supports the Creed woman being enrolled in a graduate program anywhere. Even a call to the offices of that cable program she works for didn't turn up any information.

"The surveillance tapes show the two of them examining each page of the *Gospel* with great care for several hours. I've reviewed the tapes and pulled out a section I'd like you to take a look at."

The tech officer Danislov had brought along cued the digital file and a moment later the images of Miss Creed and her companion appeared on Goshenko's monitor. It showed the man's clear agitation and what appeared to be Creed's attempt to calm him down.

"Right there," Danislov said, pointing to the

screen where the two of them were standing close together, their bodies blocking the *Gospel* from sight, "something happened. They found something, I think. I'm not sure what, for as you can see the view was obscured, but their attitudes immediately change and they become focused once more. I'm not sure what set them off, but I do know the end result."

Danislov gestured to the tech and a still image from the video appeared on the screen. In it, Annja was showing something she'd written on a pad of paper to her companion.

"Enhance that!" Goshenko snapped.

Danislov had already anticipated the request.

The four lines of text that formed a message spread themselves across the screen.

It took the colonel even less time than it had Sergeant Danislov to figure out the riddle. When he did, he snatched up the phone and barked into the receiver. "I want a security detail sent to Saint Basil's immediately. They are to secure the building, especially the main chapel, and wait for my arrival. Understood?"

Goshenko hung up without another word. He glanced at the clock on the wall, then back at Danislov. "How long has it been since Creed left Dr. Petrescu's company?"

To his credit, Danislov didn't flinch. "Three hours."

More than long enough for Creed and her companion to find "the key."

Goshenko glanced again at the four lines on the monitor and then rose to his feet. "Time to pay the Lady a visit, I think."

Ten minutes later they were standing in the central chapel inside Saint Basil's Cathedral, staring at the statue of the Virgin Mother.

Its right hand was missing.

"Go take a look," Goshenko ordered.

Danislov was not a religious man and so he had no qualms about climbing over the barrier. Pulling himself up onto the pedestal, he took a good long look at the stump at the end of the statue's wrist.

"There is a set of grooves on either side of the wrist, almost as if the hand was designed to come on and off," he told the colonel.

Goshenko opened his mouth to reply, but was interrupted by the arrival of the captain in charge of the guard detachment.

"Colonel! You should take a look at this."

The guard led them outside and over to one of the trash cans in the square. He pointed inside the mouth of the barrel.

Sitting on some discarded trash was a woman's hand.

Goshenko reached in and pulled it out, which caused the captain to recoil. But the hand wasn't flesh and blood. It was stone. The stone hand of the

Virgin Mother. The colonel looked at it for a moment and then held it up so Danislov could see the hollow center.

"I want to know what was hidden inside here, Sergeant. I don't care what you have to do, just get me whatever it was."

"Understood, sir."

Goshenko nodded, satisfied. "The American and her companion are staying over at the Marriott on Tverskaya Street. I suggest you start there."

12

The map was everything they expected it to be.

After leaving the cathedral they returned to Annja's hotel room and carefully unfolded the piece of parchment, revealing crude line drawings and notes in black ink. It only took a moment for them both to realize that it was a quickly sketched copy of the original plans for the vault, no doubt drawn by Fioravanti. While most of the text was legible, a few areas had either faded or gotten smudged out when the map was folded. It specifically noted which of the many tunnels beneath the Kremlin the construction crew had used to access the lower levels and gave directions from that point to the final location of the vault itself.

Calling it the "key to the treasure" was like saying the Hope Diamond was a nice rock.

"We did it!" Gianni cried, scooping Annja up in a hug that lifted her off her feet. Annja hugged him right back and in the process discovered a surprising set of muscles underneath his shirt. She found herself staring directly into his deep brown eyes.

"We should tell Charles, don't you think?" she said brightly, and pretended not to notice his knowing smile. Carefully he set her back down on her own two feet.

"Yes, definitely. We should get his advice on how we handle things from here on out, as well."

Gianni dug out the satellite phone and they put a call into their benefactor, but got his answering machine. Not wanting to leave any details where someone other than Charles might be able to pick them up, Annja simply said they'd had a development in their work and that he should call them back.

They spent some time going over the map, discussing key features and speculating on what the more cryptic notes might mean. Annja pulled out her camera and took several photos of the map, wanting to be able to use the computer's graphics program to enhance and enlarge the images. Maybe that would allow them to read the damaged notations a little easier. If Charles requested a copy, they would also be able to email it to him.

Deciding that a congratulatory dinner was in order, particularly since they had managed to work right through lunch that afternoon, Gianni called down to make reservations at the restaurant in the open atrium on the fifth floor.

Once Gianni had left to return to his room, Annja showered and dressed in clean clothes. In recognition of the occasion, she decided to forgo her usual T-shirt and jeans in favor of a comfortable pair of pants and a silk button-down shirt. She brushed her hair out, leaving it down for a change. A glance in the mirror, and she was ready to go.

They obtained a document tube from the business center, rolled the map up and placed it inside, and then stopped at the front desk to have it put in the hotel safe. After that, they made their way to the restaurant and asked the maître d' to seat them toward the back, away from the other diners.

Dinner tasted wonderful, though whether that was because of the chef's skill, starvation or the elation they were feeling, they couldn't say. Several times during the evening Annja caught Gianni admiring her when he thought she wasn't looking and she didn't mind the attention.

This might actually turn out to be an interesting trip, she thought to herself.

That's when she noticed the four men enter the restaurant.

They were all big men and the way they stopped just inside the entrance and surveyed the open room called attention to themselves. Their leader, a tall well-built man with a goatee and a scar on the side of his face, had a few quiet words with the maître d'. All four wore dark suits a little too small for their big frames and, as a result, Annja immediately noted the telltale bulge beneath each of their suit coats, revealing the presence of a weapon.

An uneasy feeling in her gut, Annja had the urge to reach into the otherwhere and draw her sword, wanting—no, *needing*—the protective feeling of having the weapon in hand.

That wasn't a positive sign.

She had a pretty good idea just who the men were looking for, but she needed to put it to the test before doing anything rash.

Annja waited until the newcomers had begun to fan out through the diners before turning to Gianni. "Do you see the doorway behind you?" she asked in a serious tone.

"The one to the kitchen?"

She nodded. "Get up and walk through it without looking back. Wait for me just inside the entrance. I'll catch up in a moment."

"Why on earth would I want to do that?" he asked. "Dessert just arrived and I'm enjoying myself. Aren't you?"

It would only be moments before they were spotted.

She decided being forthright in this situation was best.

"You don't want to spend the next twenty years in a Russian prison, do you?"

He began to laugh, glanced over her shoulder and

then abruptly stopped. His face blanched and he got up without another word, walked directly to the kitchen door and disappeared through it.

That caught the attention of one of the gunmen, which was exactly what Annja wanted. She hated to use Gianni as bait like that, but time was of the essence and it was the best she could come up with on short notice. The Russian apparently hadn't noticed who Gianni had been sitting with. He rushed right past Annja's table without a glance.

That, of course, was his mistake.

13

With all his attention on Gianni as he disappeared through the kitchen door, the gunman never saw Annja's foot in his path.

He stumbled, falling forward, so surprised he didn't have time to get his hands out in front of him to break his fall. His forehead hit the floor hard and loud.

Annja rose smoothly and timed her strides so that she was able to deliver a stunning kick to the gunman's face just as he rolled over and pushed himself up onto his arms. It was too much for the man's muddled mind to take and he went down.

A glance behind told her one of the other gunmen was pointing in her direction and then he called out to the other two. They were on the far side of the restaurant and not able to respond for another minute, maybe more.

It would have to be enough.

She burst through the door to find herself in the kitchen. Gianni was standing a few feet farther in the room, his hands raised before him, facing a thin man in a chef's coat and hat who was yelling in Russian and brandishing a soup ladle in Gianni's face. Annja snatched a cast-iron skillet off a nearby rack and rushed at the chef, who saw her coming out of the corner of his eye and decided that discretion might just be the better part of valor, after all. He and his staff retreated behind one of the kitchen's long counters, letting the intruders make their way across the space unhindered. There was a door on the far side of the room. Annja led Gianni through it.

A series of guest rooms lined either side of the hallway they emerged into. Annja glanced in both directions, noting a pair of elevators to her left, the stairwell to her right and the maid's cart in the middle of the hallway in between. She thought longingly about the backpack she'd left in the room upstairs, the one containing her camera and laptop. She didn't want to leave it behind, but going up instead of down seemed like a bad idea from a tactical perspective, especially if their pursuers knew who they were. Getting cornered in the hallways above wasn't something she wanted to experience. Which left only one option—down.

"Come on!" she shouted, racing down the hallway toward the elevator, Gianni at her heels. As she passed the maid's cart she noticed that two of the hotel rooms were open and in the process of being cleared, but the maids themselves were nowhere in sight.

The open rooms gave her an idea.

They reached the elevator and Annja slapped the call button. The doors to the left-hand elevator opened at once, as if it had been sitting there, waiting for them. Gianni moved to step inside but Annja stopped him with an outstretched arm.

"No," she said sharply. "We're not taking the elevator."

As he watched, she leaned in, stabbed the button for the first floor and let the doors close on an empty elevator.

"Get inside that room," she said, pushing him back the way they had come, her gaze on the door to the kitchen.

They had seconds left, at best....

They had just stepped inside the room and eased the door shut behind them when they heard the kitchen door slam open and rough voices. Annja didn't speak Russian, but she hoped the shouts she was hearing meant they had seen the light over the elevator door flashing.

A moment passed and then she heard the ding as the doors on the second bank of elevators opened. There was some commotion, each talking over the other, and then silence as, no doubt, the elevator began its descent.

"Are they gone?" Gianni whispered in her ear. It was only then that Annja realized she had him pinned against the wall behind her, her body pressed back against his as she cracked open the door a little and peeked out.

She eased off him, turned in his direction and held a finger to her lips. When he nodded, she slowly eased the door open farther and looked out into the hallway.

It was empty.

She grabbed Gianni's hand and pulled him out with her, heading for the exit sign over a door in the middle of the corridor. Her plan was to take that down to the basement where they could hopefully find an alternate exit out of the hotel and avoid any further confrontation with their pursuers.

It was a good plan.

She just hadn't counted on the sudden appearance of the first gunman, the one she'd put down with a judiciously placed kick inside the restaurant, as he stumbled out of the door from the kitchen.

Annja didn't think. She grabbed the maid's cart and rushed it down the corridor, shouting to Gianni as she went. "The stairs! Get to the stairs!"

The gunman, still groggy from the first encounter he'd had with Annja, didn't have his gun out, which ultimately saved their lives. The maid's cart would have been minimal protection if he started firing at them. As it was he fumbled to get his gun out of his shoulder holster and in the end that proved to be his undoing. He was just pulling it free when the cart slammed into him, forcing him back through the doorway to the kitchen and off his feet once more.

Annja turned and sprinted for the stairwell, bursting through the door to find an anxious Gianni waiting there for her.

"Head down the stairs," she said, pointing for emphasis. "Don't be afraid to make noise. I want him to pay attention to you rather than me."

"What are you going to be doing?"

"Hopefully making sure he doesn't follow us again. Now go!"

Thankfully he had learned his lesson in the restaurant and didn't question her. His steps echoed up the stairwell as he went.

Annja whirled around and ran up the stairs rather than down, rounding the landing and moving a few steps up the next section of stairwell until she was confident she wouldn't be seen from the stairwell door below. She pressed her back against the wall, out of sight, then she reached into the otherwhere and drew her sword, holding it upright before her as she waited for the gunman's arrival.

He came crashing through the door just as she'd expected, the noise he made echoing through the stairwell. It also covered up the sound of Gianni's footsteps, forcing the gunman to stand still for a moment and let the noise he made fade before he could decide whether his quarry had gone up or down. Annja used those precious few seconds to plan out her next move, getting ready for what was to come. She was only going to get one chance....

The minute she could hear Gianni's footsteps again, she went into action, rushing to the landing. There she planted one hand against the railing and vaulted over it, dropping toward the gunman's unprotected back as he headed down in pursuit of Gianni.

Her feet struck him between the shoulder blades, driving him downward so that for a second she was balanced on his back, riding him like a surfer rides a wave, and then she jumped clear, not wanting to become tangled up with him as he fell. She landed lightly, the additional dexterity the sword seemed to impart on her helping her keep her balance. She was ready to face her opponent should he regain his feet quicker than she expected.

Except this time their pursuer wasn't going to get back up. He slammed into the next landing at an odd angle and Annja could clearly hear the crack as his neck broke, leaving his head at an impossible angle, staring up at her with sightless eyes.

She swore beneath her breath.

She hadn't intended to kill him, it being awfully difficult to question a corpse, but there was nothing to be done about it now. Conscious that the others might have realized their mistake and already be looking for them, Annja didn't waste any time with regrets. She knelt beside the body and quickly searched it for some kind of credentials or identification, something to let her know who was after them. But she came up empty.

Shaking her head in disgust at how quickly things had gone totally to hell, she headed down the stairs after Gianni.

14

She found him waiting for her in front of the door
that led to the first floor and visible relief washed
across him as she came into view. He moved to open
the door but she shook her head, pointing past him to
the rest of the stairwell that led to the lower floors,
no doubt the haven of the service personnel who,
on any given day, catered to the needs of the hotel's
nine hundred guests.

Their pursuers would be waiting for them in the
lobby. Or at least that's what she would have done
if she were them. Leave one or two of their number to watch the lobby, make sure those they were
pursuing didn't emerge from a different elevator or
stairwell, while the rest of the team began to can-
vas other floors.

Doing something unexpected, like bypassing the
quick route to the street in favor of heading deeper

into the hotel, might throw off the pursuit and give them extra time to get away unobserved.

Or so she hoped.

The stairs ended one floor below and when they stepped out of the stairwell they found themselves in a wide corridor in the heart of the hotel's service area. Several men in blue coveralls were pushing carts of dirty linens in one direction while the next shift of maids were busy stocking their carts from an open supply closet. Annja and Gianni slipped out into the flow of traffic, following the men with the laundry carts, hoping to find an exit.

Near the end of the hall was a set of double doors on the right, both of which were propped open, letting the occasional wave of steam out. Annja caught the heavy scent of detergent and bleach and steered Gianni in that direction, assuming that there would have to be some decent ventilation in the room to keep the workers from becoming overcome by the chemicals. The easiest way to do that was to have a door to the outside.

They were just about to go in when a man shouted from behind them. "Stop!"

The voice was full of command authority and everyone, Annja and Gianni included, responded to it, instinctively turning in that direction.

It was the leader of the gunmen, Annja saw immediately. He stood in the middle of the hallway, having just come out of the elevator at the far end.

That narrow face and goatee stood out. As did his charcoal-gray suit. And the gun in his hand.

The gun he was pointing at them.

"Run!" Annja yelled.

Screaming erupted as several of the hotel staff realized there was a man with a gun in their midst and they were between him and his target. Chaos ensued. Staff scattered in every direction, carts and laundry went flying as people fought to find cover. Gianni shot into the laundry room, Annja on his heels.

Massive industrial washing machines lined one side of the room, dryers the other. Employees were standing, wondering what all the commotion was about and staring curiously at the civilians in their midst.

"Vykhod?" Annja asked, hoping she was getting the pronunciation right, thankful for the dozen or so words in Russian she'd memorized on the flight over.

Several of the workers turned and pointed to the far end of the room, where an open door was half-hidden behind several wrapped bundles of laundry.

"Spasibo!" Annja yelled over her shoulder as they ran for the exit.

She and Gianni burst out the door to find themselves in a dimly lit alley at the back of the hotel. Annja didn't hesitate, just grabbed Gianni by the hand and took off down the alley at a dead run, their footsteps echoing off the walls around them as she dragged him along in her wake. She was praying that they'd reach the other end before their pursuers caught up with them, knowing that they'd be gunned down like ducks in a shooting gallery if they didn't.

The alley opened up onto a side street that was just as dark and just as empty. Annja didn't stop there, either; she raced down that one until it bisected a slightly more trafficked area. Cars were parked up and down the road—Ladas, Charkas and even a few Volvos and Mercedes—but there were no people. With her hand still clamped over Gianni's, she led them across the street and then ducked down behind the nearest automobile.

Gianni was about to say something but she quickly stopped him with her hand over his mouth.

"Shh! Listen."

Behind them she could hear shouting and the sharp sound of footfalls against the pavement.

They weren't out of this yet.

Annja glanced down the street. Traffic was moving on the next street, but it was a long way off. It would take them several minutes to get there and even then there was no guarantee they would find cover. The buildings lining the street were either apartment buildings with thick iron gates, no doubt locked tight at this hour, or commercial properties with their doors hidden behind steel shutters and thick chains.

Clearly the cars lining the street were their best bet.

Annja began to creep along beside the cars in a

low squat, being sure to keep her head below window level and therefore out of sight of anyone coming down the street they'd just left behind.

Gianni crept along behind her, casting nervous glances back over his shoulder every few seconds. "Now what?"

Annja ignored him, intent on her search. She needed something nondescript but also something with enough guts under the hood to get them away from their pursuers. She wasn't familiar enough with the Russian models to even make an educated guess as to their usefulness. Fortunately, there was a black Mercedes sedan parked three cars up.

She crept beside it and gently lifted the handle on the front passenger door.

Locked.

"What are you doing?" Gianni whispered in her ear.

"Getting us out of here," Annja whispered back as she glanced up and down the street.

Not seeing anyone, she rose to her feet, put her back to the door and smashed her elbow sharply against the driver's-side window. The sound of the glass shattering was still hanging in the air as she reached in and opened the door.

"Get in and keep your head down," she said.

"But…"

"No buts!" she snarled. "Get in before we're out of time."

As if to emphasize her point, they heard the sound of a shot and a bullet shattered the window of the car parked behind them.

That was all the urging Gianni needed. He hauled open the back door and flung himself down on the backseat as Annja climbed into the front.

Shouts were coming from somewhere behind them now but she ignored them, kicking savagely at the steering column until the portion covering the ignition wires cracked away.

"Get us out of here!" Gianni yelled from the backseat.

Annja didn't waste her breath in replying, but that was exactly what she *was* doing. She slid in behind the wheel and then reached under the steering column. She yanked down the wires and quickly selected the ones she needed.

More sounds of gunfire, much closer this time, and bullets slammed into the trunk of the car, causing Gianni to let loose a blistering stream of curses in Italian. Thankfully none of the bullets came through into the passenger compartment. Annja chanced a glance behind her and saw three men closing in on their position. They had guns in their hands and even as she looked on, one of them fired again, the bullet blowing a hole in the rear window and plowing into the headrest of the passenger seat only a few inches away from her face.

She twisted the wires together in her hand and

was rewarded with the throaty growl of the Mercedes engine. With a shout of triumph she cut the wheel to the left, threw the gearshift into drive and hit the accelerator. The Mercedes rocked away from the curb, its tires squealing.

Bullets chased them down the street.

"WE NEED TO DITCH THE CAR," Gianni said.

He was right. It had been an hour since their narrow escape from the hotel and sooner or later someone was sure to report the car as stolen, if it hadn't happened already. Frankly she was surprised they'd attracted as little attention as they had; apparently the sight of a vehicle with enough bullet holes in it to play connect-the-dots wasn't as uncommon a sight to the citizens of Moscow as she'd imagined it would be.

She'd been driving aimlessly for the past hour, trying to stay off the main thoroughfares and threading her way through the back streets, intentionally avoiding those nicer parts of the city that foreigners like them would be most expected to retreat to in times of trouble. Now she'd begun intentionally looking for a place where they could leave the Mercedes behind without getting mugged or killed in the process.

She found it about fifteen minutes later, a rundown neighborhood of tenement buildings and corner bars but with enough foot traffic that they wouldn't be mugged the minute they abandoned the vehicle. Annja parked between a battered old Volvo and a panel truck that had seen better days. They left the doors unlocked and just walked away, knowing the car wouldn't be there by sunrise and feeling pretty happy about that. The chop-shop thieves would tear it down to its component parts in a matter of hours, erasing any evidence of their theft in the process.

They walked to the nearest bar and paid the bartender six hundred rubles, or about twenty bucks American, to have him call them a cab. It was highway robbery, no doubt about it, but Annja couldn't afford to call attention to themselves by arguing— or threatening the bartender with her sword—so she let it go.

She thanked him for his generosity in making the call as she handed over the money. The whole time she was telling herself that karma always has a way of coming back and biting you on the ass when you least expect it and that bartender was going to get his own, no doubt about it.

The cabbie thought they were a couple of rich tourists out slumming and he also tried to gouge them. This time they were away from prying eyes and Annja quickly disabused him of the notion with a few choice words and a highly effective nerve strike to the arm she had snatched up and was now holding over the back of the seat. For a moment she thought she was going to have to snap the arm, which might give her satisfaction but wouldn't get them out of their current predicament, but then the cabbie gave in and took them to a nearby hotel without any more fuss.

It was the kind of place that rented rooms by the hour and charged a deposit on the bedsheets, but Annja didn't care at this point. Everyone who came here was looking for some privacy and those who stayed made an effort not to remember anything about anyone else they might see. Still, it was only when they were both safely behind the door of the single room they had rented for the night, clutching their sheets, that Annja began to breathe a little easier.

Because they had been waiting for Sir Charles Davies to return their call, Gianni had been carrying the satellite phone with him at dinner. Thankfully it had survived the subsequent chase and gun battle. They used it now to call their benefactor.

Charles answered on the second ring.

"Annja! I hear you have good news for me."

It's amazing what a few hours can do to change one's fortunes, she thought before taking the time to explain everything that had happened that afternoon and evening. It was not a brief conversation.

"Where are you now?" he asked, once she had finished bringing him up to speed.

"A run-down hotel on the outskirts of town."

"And the map?"

"Still locked in the safe at the Marriott, as far as I know."

"Which means whoever is chasing you may or may not have it."

"I'd guess the latter. It will take them time to make the connection between our faces and the names of a couple of registered guests, so there might be time to recover it."

That earned her a grunt from him. "It's far too dangerous for you to even try," he said to her. "I'll see if I can have someone pick it up in proxy for you in the morning. In the meantime, lay low until you hear from me tomorrow. It's going to take some time to work out a way to get you to the American Embassy."

"The embassy?" Annja asked. "Whatever for?"

"To help get you out of the country, of course. You've got armed gunmen after you, Annja. Clearly the situation has gotten too dangerous."

Annja laughed. She couldn't help it. She had managed to find the first clue to the location of the Library of Gold since it had disappeared five hundred years ago and he wanted her to give it up?

"Why are you laughing?"

"I'm not backing down—not a chance. I studied that map long enough I can practically re-create it from memory. I'm sure I can. You figure out a way for us to get into those tunnels and I'll find you that library."

She noticed Gianni looking at her oddly, so she asked Charles to hold on for a moment and covered the receiver with her hand.

"What?" she asked him.

"Have you gone mad?"

"Of course not."

"Then why are you telling him that we're going after the library?"

"Because I am—I assumed you'd want to come with me. Was I wrong?"

After what seemed like an eternity, he finally nodded.

It seemed straightforward to her. The only way to ensure nothing they had done so far would come back to haunt them in the end was to continue the expedition. The authorities would be forced to recognize them for finding and restoring such a valuable piece of Russian history. And if there was one thing Annja had learned over the years, it was that it is awfully hard to publicly arrest a hero.

She put the phone back to her ear. "So what's our next step?"

"I'm not sure yet. Stay in your hotel room for now. That will minimize your chances of being seen and recognized. I'll make some calls, see what I can figure out. I'll get back to you as soon as I have something."

They said their goodbyes and hung up.

It looked like it was going to be a long night for all of them.

15

Annja spent a restless night in that cramped little hotel room, lying beside Gianni on the narrow bed. The Italian slept like the dead, snoring quietly in her ear, but several times Annja awoke to voices in the hall. When she did, she'd lie there in nervous anticipation, ready to call her sword and use it if need be. But each time the voices faded as the speakers moved away down the hall.

Annja was up with the dawn, pacing back and forth inside the small room, staring at the satellite phone and willing it to ring despite the fact that it was the middle of the night in the U.S. She hated sitting around, waiting on someone else. She was a doer by nature and wanted to be figuring out mysteries on her own. But she was hampered by her lack of contacts in this part of the world, never mind the restrictiveness of the regime that controlled the area they needed to be searching in.

She'd come to the conclusion that even if they were being chased by members of a government agency, which she believed they were, then those members were not acting in any kind of official capacity. Otherwise, the men back at the restaurant would have identified themselves and would have had people watching the entrance and exits to the hotel to be sure they wouldn't escape. Which meant it was a private group or individual after them. That the gunman she'd taken out hadn't had any official ID supported her theory.

And they were not afraid to use force to get what they wanted.

But what, exactly, did they want?

That was the question she couldn't yet answer. She suspected it had to do with the map and, by extension, the library. Though she didn't understand how word had leaked out about it. Perhaps one of Charles's contacts had been loose-lipped?

Of course, there was also the possibility that whoever was after them had nothing at all to do with the library, that it was Annja who was the target over something to do with a confrontation in her past. Since taking up the sword she'd foiled the plans of some dangerous people and there was nothing yet to prove that this wasn't revenge against her.

For all she knew, they might have even been after Gianni. She barely knew him and had no idea what kinds of activities he might have been involved in prior to this.

Trouble was, until they knew more about who it was chasing them, there was no way to tell.

It was a decidedly irritating situation.

To help pass the time, Annja tried to re-create Fioravanti's map from memory. She found a phone book in the nightstand even though there wasn't a phone in the room. She tore the cover off it and used the blank space on the inside to sketch out the map and as many of the notations as she could remember. It wasn't perfect, but it was close and would at least get them within the general vicinity of the vault.

Gianni finally woke up around nine, just as she was finishing the map. The guests on each floor shared a single, communal bathroom, one without a shower, no less. The two of them took turns standing outside the door while the other had a quick sponge bath.

Annja had dealt with worse conditions and didn't mind, but Gianni grumbled the entire time. Annja thought about giving him some grief over it, but decided to be merciful. It was probably his first time being chased by armed gunmen, after all, and a little mercy might make the day go easier.

By lunch there was still no word from Charles Davies and the cramped confines of the hotel room were wearing on them considerably. Annja was confident they hadn't been followed to the hotel last night, and given her belief that they weren't officially wanted by the police, she figured they were safe enough to slip out and grab a bite to eat, provided they didn't linger in the open. They managed to get the location of a café from the recalcitrant hotel clerk and five minutes later were seated at an outside table, sipping coffee and waiting on their sandwiches and, in Gianni's case, a side of French fries. Gianni had the satellite phone so they wouldn't miss Charles when he called and it rested on the table, the ringer set to high.

They were halfway through with their lunch when a stranger pulled out the chair between them and sat down at their table. Annja froze with her fork partway to her mouth.

He was a big man, in both height and weight. He reminded her of one of those Russian weightlifters she'd seen in the Olympics, heavy muscle layered over a big frame. His head was shaved smooth, his eyes were a dark brown and he had a cauliflower ear that threw off the rounded symmetry of his face.

He was dressed simply in dark blue coveralls worn over a thermal shirt that had once been white and was now closer to ivory with a hint of battleship gray.

"Good morning, my American friends," he exclaimed. With an impish grin, he stole a French fry off Gianni's plate.

Annja wasn't buying the "I'm harmless" act, not for an instant. She casually put her fork down and let her right hand fall below the level of the table, where it would be out of sight if she had to draw her sword. She could call the weapon to her and shove it into the stranger's guts before *he* could draw a weapon. That knowledge alone allowed her to breathe easier for the moment.

The Russian had spoken English, but Annja gave no sign that she understood that language. She replied in a torrent of French, taking him to task for his rudeness at interrupting their lunch, not wanting to betray that she, at least, was an American. Until she knew who he was and just what he wanted from them.

Across the table Gianni was getting ready to take some action of his own, though what he was intending to do Annja didn't know. Apparently the newcomer sensed the pending explosion, as well. He lifted his meaty hands off the table and held them before his chest in a gesture of surrender.

"Easy now," he said, still sticking with English even if his mastery of the language wasn't perfect. "Sir Charles said you may be a little jumpy. No need to get upset. I'm only here to help."

As if on cue, the satellite phone in the middle of the table chose that moment to begin ringing.

They all turned and stared at it.

"You going to get that?" the Russian asked.

Annja glared at him. "How do you know Sir Charles Davies?" she asked in English.

Their guest gestured at the still-ringing phone. "Answer the phone." He smiled in what Annja guessed he intended to be a reassuring manner.

In truth he looked more like a grimacing frog, but she snatched up the phone, anyway.

"Hello?" Annja got up from the table and took a few steps away.

"How is everything there, Annja? Are you and Gianni doing all right?"

"We're fine, if you ignore the big Russian with the wrestler's ear who's claiming to know you and interrupting our lunch."

Charles laughed. "He's there already? I'm happy to hear I can add efficiency to his list of many talents."

Annja eyed the man who had been sitting across from her, slightly mollified now that Charles had corroborated sending him. "I'd say that's a good thing, if I had any idea what he's doing here."

"His name is Vladimir Vikofsky and he is going to get you underground. That is, of course, if you are still interested in pursuing the library."

"You know I am. Tell me about our new friend."

"He's the leader of a group that calls itself the Urban Underground, whose stated aim is to study the historical, ecological and social aspects of the Moscow underground. Personally, I think he just gets a kick out of exploring places he's not supposed to be."

I like him already, Annja thought. "I've heard

of the Urban Underground. Had help from them in the past."

"Good. And don't let Vladimir's size and laidback manner fool you. He's a veritable genius when it comes to moving around down there. If there is anyone on the planet who can get you to where you need to be, he's the one. You can talk about the library freely with him. I'm confident in his discretion."

"All right. I think we can live with that."

"How's Gianni holding up?"

"Just fine," she said, glancing over to see him watching Vikofsky the way one might watch a small but temperamental dog, as if uncertain if it was going to suddenly go nuts and bite you.

"Let me know if you think he's having difficulties. You are far more used to this kind of thing than he is."

"I'm sure he'll rise to the occasion." Annja believed it, too. Most people would have cracked under the pressure of what they'd gone through the evening before but he'd slept through the night—even when she hadn't.

Annja agreed to check in with Charles the next morning, once they knew exactly how they intended to move forward, after which they said their goodbyes and she then rejoined the others at the table.

Annja made the introductions, then made sure Vladimir understood what they were looking for.

"There are six levels of tunnel under Moscow,

perhaps as many as twelve," he told them. "Old sewer systems, fountain foundations, drainage tunnels, rerouted streams and underground river systems, subway tunnels and access systems. I have mapped the first three completely. I can take you where you need to be."

Annja knew Moscow had been built along the swampy banks of the Moskva River. Workers quickly discovered that the soil was soft and pliable, the kind that easily gives way to a determined man with a shovel. As the village grew into a city, expanding outward, it also grew downward. Paranoid czars built underground bunkers and vaults to hide their treasures and to provide protection from unexpected attacks. Subsequent rulers had followed in Ivan the Terrible's path, bending the underground to their will. In the late 1700s, Catherine the Great had decided she didn't like the location of the Neglina River and had brought in architects to divert its entire length into a vast underground network of brick-lined tunnels where it still runs today. Under Stalin the Soviets had dug even deeper, building secret tunnels, fallout shelters and KGB listening posts.

The idea that they might make use of the underground to reach the vault rather than descending through the Kremlin itself was a good one and Annja was frankly surprised she hadn't come up with that solution herself.

Seeing they had another guest, the waiter approached, but Annja waved him off.

"Let me see this map you have," Vikofsky said, holding out his hand.

"We don't have it anymore."

"Where is it?"

Annja explained what had happened the night before and the reason they were holed up at the hotel down the street rather than back at the Marriott.

"You think the map is still in the hotel safe?" Vikofsky asked.

She shrugged. She had no way of knowing and was hesitant to call the hotel in case someone had put two and two together and could identify her and Gianni as the guests involved in the shoot-out last night. She said as much to Vikofsky.

"We should go see," he replied. "I know someone behind the desk who will check for me. Cost me price of dinner, but she is nice girl."

"I'm willing to try if you are."

"You're as crazy as she is," Gianni muttered. Annja and Vladimir smiled at each other.

This might just work out, after all, Annja thought.

16

Vlad, as he preferred to be called, drove a slate-gray Volkswagen minibus so covered with graffiti that it looked like a throwback to the seventies. The three of them piled in—Vladimir behind the wheel, Annja riding shotgun and Gianni sitting between the two seats on a plastic milk crate shanghaied into service as a makeshift chair. The engine fired up with a cough and a bang that did nothing to reassure either of the two passengers that it could actually get them from point A to point B without breaking down at least half a dozen times.

Their Russian friend seemed unconcerned, however, so Annja did her best to ignore it. Vlad was a spastic, though adept, driver and negotiated the busy city streets with a deftness that spoke of long practice. Almost before Annja knew it they were entering the center of the city.

Vlad drove past the Marriott and pulled the van to

the curb a couple of blocks farther down the street.
He watched the entrance of the hotel through his
side mirror for several minutes. Satisfied, he said,
"Wait here," and hopped out of the van, leaving the
engine running.

As soon as he turned away, Annja slid over into
the driver's seat, ready to take charge of the Volkswagen if they needed to leave in a hurry. She watched
him through the side-view mirror as he made his
way across the busy street and disappeared inside
the Marriott.

Let's just hope he comes out again, she thought
to herself.

SERGEANT ARKADY DANISLOV was likewise holed up
in a vehicle, watching the entrance to the Marriott, though the Mercedes sedan he'd been loaned for
the duration of the assignment was decidedly more
comfortable than the Volkswagen Annja and her
companion were waiting in up the street.

The night before had been a disaster and Danislov
was still berating himself for the mistakes he'd made.
He'd wrongly assumed that the Creed woman wasn't
a threat and so he and his men had been unprepared
for the level of response. It had taken Danislov hours
to clean up the mess and he'd had to invoke his authority as an agent of the Federal Security Service,
or FSS, several times, declaring the entire incident a
matter of national security in order to keep the Mos-

cow police out of the mess. Goshenko hadn't been happy, but he had let Danislov deal with it his way without interference.

It had been a long night and more than anything else Danislov wanted to go home and get some sleep, but he had a hunch that Annja Creed might return to the hotel to get her belongings. And he wanted to be here if she did. He'd intentionally left her hotel room alone for that very reason, not wanting to reveal his hand. His men hadn't been carrying any ID last night, so right now she probably suspected she'd inadvertently become tied up in some kind of failed kidnapping, perhaps by the Russian mafia or some other criminal organization. Such events had become increasingly common over the past several years, after all.

The blare of a car horn brought him out of his reverie and he looked out the window to see a burly man in coveralls and a backpack slung over his shoulder crossing the street with little regard for the traffic moving in either direction.

"Jackass," he said, and then turned away to watch the entrance to the hotel.

ANNJA HAD BEGUN TO GROW concerned, thinking Vlad had been inside the hotel too long only to recover something from the safe, when she heard the blare of a horn and saw him cutting across traffic toward them.

She slid over to her own seat and a moment later Vlad opened the door and climbed inside, holding her backpack. He passed it over with that crazy grin on his face.

"No problem. Got the pack *and* the map, plus date for Friday night."

Annja couldn't believe it. She unzipped the pack and looked inside. Her laptop and digital camera were there, along with the document tube in which they'd placed the map. "How on earth…?"

"My friend also has passkey to guest rooms," he said, still grinning. "Thought you might want your computer back, too."

"I do, thanks." It was a pleasant surprise and she appreciated his forethought, but still, it was troubling.

"There wasn't any problem getting the pack out of the room?"

Vlad shook his head as he pulled out into traffic. "No problem. Friend said big incident last night with the FSS, but it was hushed up and she did not have details. You wouldn't be knowing anything about that now, would you?"

The FSS? Those men last night had been with the Federal Security Service?

That was going to complicate things. The FSS had access to all kinds of surveillance information coming out of traffic cameras, bank ATMs, private security systems, you name it. It could make it very difficult for them to move around the city. Never mind how difficult it would be to get out of the country if an official alert for their arrest and apprehension was put out.

Somehow the FSS must have connected them to the damaged statue in the cathedral, though why that would be an issue for the former KGB was beyond her. It seemed more like something the Moscow police would handle.

If the men chasing them last night had been FSS agents on official business, why hadn't they identified themselves?

Instinct told her there was something else going on.

Without any way to get to the bottom of it at the moment, she pushed it to the back of her mind to mull over later. "Where are we going?"

"World headquarters for the Urban Underground," Vlad told her.

As it turned out, the headquarters for the world-famous Urban Underground turned out to be a dingy flat on the second floor of a crumbling old apartment building.

Vlad's flat, actually.

One he shared with his aging mother.

He helped the old woman into her bedroom, turned on her television and got her a cup of hot tea, before joining Annja and Gianni in the front room.

The space had been converted into a kind of

makeshift office. Annja stood in the center of the room, staring at the hundreds of hand-drawn maps that decorated the white-painted walls like its own kind of graffiti. They had been drawn to resemble three-dimensional cutaway plans, so that one could see the relationships between one level and the next at a glance. The level of detail was astounding and Annja was suddenly very pleased that Charles had managed to track Vikofsky down and enlist him in their adventure. He was going to be an invaluable resource for helping them navigate the underground in search of the vault.

"Map, please," he said to her, and Annja handed it over without hesitation. Vlad opened the document tube, carefully pulled out the map and then unrolled it on the table. He routed around in a drawer for a few minutes until he found the jeweler's loop he was looking for. He spent long moments studying the drawings and the annotations on its surface, muttering to himself in Russian, and then walked over to one wall, comparing the information on the map with several of the drawings there. Clearly unsatisfied, he moved to a second section of drawings and then a third. Gianni was casting disparaging glances in Vlad's direction, but Annja ignored him, not yet willing to give up on the big Russian.

Then, all of the sudden, Vlad gave a low whoop and tapped the wall hard with his fist.

He turned to face them.

"Who wants to go exploring?"

17

After watching the hotel entrance all night, Danislov had turned the duty over to a subordinate and returned to his apartment for a few hours of sleep. He awoke feeling refreshed and ready to take on the challenge ahead of him—finding two fugitives in a city of more than ten million people.

The best thing, he knew, was to start at the beginning. In this case that meant a visit to the offices of the Federal Migration Service.

His FSS credentials allowed him to cut through the red tape and, within minutes of arriving, he was ensconced in a cubicle with a pert little platinum-blond aide who had been ordered to give him whatever he needed.

"I want to see the entrance records for Annja Creed," Danislov told her. He gave her the date he believed Creed had entered the country, but it really wasn't necessary. The massive database the Federal

Migration Service, or FMS, kept on every individual who crossed the nation's borders was more than sophisticated enough to find the records he wanted with just a name. But adding the date would allow them to cull the records into something more manageable if she had made more than one visit in the past several months.

As it turned out, she hadn't visited Moscow very often. On this particular trip, Miss Creed had arrived in Moscow the night before the incident at Saint Basil's. The records showed that she and Gianni Travino had arrived on Aeroflot 861 and had subsequently been detained together for a short time while passing through immigration.

Danislov had the aide call up what information they had on Travino, which wasn't much. He entered Russia with an Italian passport that listed his legal residence as an address in Rome and his occupation as an artist. This corresponded to what Dr. Petrescu had told him. The woman, Creed, had come to study the text of the *Gospel of Gold* while her male companion, whose name Petrescu had either missed or forgotten, had been there to examine the artwork adorning the *Gospel*'s pages.

It sounded suspicious to Danislov. An artist? Who actually tried to support himself as an artist in this day and age? He suspected Travino's occupation was actually a cover for something else, but Danislov hadn't been with the Federal Security Service long enough to be able to ferret that out.

No matter, he thought. I've got their names and descriptions, which is all I really need to issue an alert. Half the city would be looking for them moments after he did that. That would make it difficult for Creed and Travino to move freely in the city and hamper any actions they might take to locate the library, which would not make Colonel Goshenko happy.

In the end, that was the only thing that really mattered to Danislov. When Goshenko was happy, Danislov's life was considerably easier.

His attention returned to the notation that Creed and her companion had been detained upon arrival. There wasn't any indication of what had happened to require the FMS officers to do so—just a quick note that they had been detained for questioning.

Curious, he had the aide write down the home number for the shift supervisor from that day, a man named Yuri Basilovich. Perhaps he could shed some light on the issue.

Danislov also had her print out copies of the fugitives' passport photos, then thanked her for her help and headed back to his office in the Kremlin. There he gathered the twenty-five men Goshenko had placed at his command and divided them into teams of five. Each team member was given copies of the passport photos and then the teams were assigned various sectors around the city and sent to begin searching.

The chance that any of them would actually strike gold and stumble upon the fugitives was slim, but it was better than doing nothing.

Once everyone was gone, he pulled out the phone number he'd gotten from the aide and moments later had Mr. Basilovich on the phone. The conversation was short but not very sweet, at least not for the immigration supervisor. When Basilovich tried to dither in his answers, Danislov had no choice but to threaten him with reassignment to Ulaanbaatar, Mongolia. Danislov himself didn't have anything against Mongolia; it was simply the first place he could think of in the moment.

Basilovich cracked like an egg, revealing why he had been reluctant to answer Danislov's questions.

He was a fan.

A *Chasing History's Monsters* fan. The biggest one in all of Russia, he proclaimed with enthusiasm.

Danislov had been hoping Creed had said or done something suspicious, something they could use to build a case against her if they were required to do so at a later time. Instead, he'd gotten the blatherings of a lovesick idiot.

But then Basilovich said something useful.

"I bet that laptop is full of information about whatever she's searching for now. I'd give anything to see what's on it."

Laptop...whatever she's searching for now.

Danislov hung up without another word, snatched the photos of Creed and Travino off his desk and dashed out of his office. The Marriott was only a few blocks away so he didn't bother with his department-issue vehicle, making the trip on foot instead, berating himself the entire time. He'd been watching the hotel for their return, but hadn't thought of examining their belongings for information relative to the search for the library.

You're an idiot, Danislov.

Once at the Marriott he summoned the manager, flashed his credentials and asked to be let into the fugitives' rooms. The manager was used to keeping the FSS, and before them the KGB, happy and didn't hesitate in providing access to each of the adjoining rooms.

He started with Creed's, which, as it turned out, didn't take long because she hadn't bothered to unpack. She was living out of her suitcase, as if expecting to leave at a moment's notice. Even her toiletries—soap, shampoo, toothbrush and toothpaste—were still inside one of her roller bag's outer pockets.

In contrast, Travino's room looked as if he intended to stay awhile. His clothes were neatly put away in the drawers of the armoire and his shaving kit and other toiletries were carefully arranged in the bathroom.

Nowhere, however, did Danislov find a backpack with a laptop in it.

Perhaps she put them in the hotel safe, he thought, and returned to the front desk a second time.

After checking the records, the manager said, "Yes, Miss Creed did place something in the safe recently, but it was retrieved a few hours ago."

"Retrieved?"

"Yes. She sent a courier with signed authorization and the proper ID for a pickup earlier today."

Danislov cursed and headed for the front door, angry with himself for not thinking of this sooner. He'd been right here, watching the entrance when the courier had come in, he guessed. He had inadvertently let their best lead slip from their fingers without even knowing it was happening right under his nose.

He had just stepped outside when his cell phone rang.

"Danislov."

"We've got them, sir. We've got them!"

Danislov knew the caller was one of his search team leaders but didn't know which one.

"Identify yourself and where you are."

"Lieutenant Chernov, sir. We're in Manege Square, sir. The fugitives and another man, a Russian national from the looks of him, are entering the ventilation shaft on Doheni Prospeckt. We're going to follow them."

"What? Wait! I want you to…"

There was a beep and the line went dead.

What the…?

"Yebat!" he yelled savagely, and nearly smashed the phone on the ground. An elderly woman walking nearby gave him a dirty look.

Manege Square was on the far side of the Kremlin, adjacent to Red Square. It wasn't more than a twenty-minute walk on a good day.

Danislov took off down the street at a run, cursing his earlier decision to leave his staff car behind.

18

Two hours after deciding to continue the search, Annja, Gianni and Vladimir were back in the Volkswagen minivan, headed for a sidewalk ventilation shaft near the crumbling remains of what had once been Moscow State University in Manege Square.

Back in the fifties, the main university had relocated to Sparrow Hill in southwest Moscow, leaving only a handful of faculty buildings operational at the original site a few blocks from the Kremlin. Vlad assured them that they would be able to slip into the underground without a lot of difficulty. From there they would descend two levels while gradually making their way south about half a mile, until they reached the starting point designated on Fioravanti's map.

It sounded like a plan to Annja.

She sat up front, dressed in clothes borrowed from a female friend of Vladimir's. The jeans were a little too long and the knitted sweater hung loosely

on her athletic frame, but Annja knew how cool it
could be underground and she was glad to have the
warmer clothing.

At least I'm not swimming in my clothes, she
thought with a glance in Gianni's direction. He was
wearing borrowed clothing, too, both of them having lost their luggage in their rapid departure from
their hotel. The normally well-dressed Italian was
not happy about it, either.

After a half-hour drive Vlad pulled into a narrow
alley behind several decrepit-looking buildings. He
parked the van right up along the sidewalk to block
anyone passing by from getting a good view of the
grate covering the ventilation shaft only a few feet
away. He pocketed the keys and turned to his companions.

"Time to suit up," he told them.

For Vlad, that meant donning a dirty yellow fireman's jacket, a battered motorcycle helmet without
a visor and a pair of rubber wading boots that made
Annja want to gag at the smell. He pulled similar
gear from the back of the van for Annja and Gianni.

"You're kidding, right?" Gianni asked, staring
in dismay at the horrible green boots he'd just been
given.

Vlad laughed and slapped Gianni on the back
hard enough to make him stagger. "You look good
in boots!" Vlad exclaimed. "Like real member of
Urban Underground."

While Annja and Gianni got dressed in the relative cover of the van, Vlad strapped headlamps to their spelunkers' helmets, checked to be sure the batteries were fresh and stashed extra sets in the pockets of his voluminous coat.

It wouldn't do to be a few hundred feet beneath the surface and run out of light, Annja thought as she watched him.

Wouldn't do at all.

He gave each of them a small waist pack containing four chemical light sticks, two bottles of water and a handful of granola bars. He slung a nylon climbing rope—just in case, he told them—over one shoulder and, last but not least, grabbed a hefty iron crowbar from a bucket of them in the back of the van.

Vlad scanned the street, double-checking that they were alone. The van would be picked up by another member of the Urban Underground, but for now it kept what they were about to do from wandering eyes. He jammed one end of the crowbar between the bars of the grate, turned it to set the hook and then pulled the end of the grate up a good three feet off the ground.

"Quickly!" he said. "Down the ladder."

Annja found herself descending a carbonate-encrusted ladder that looked as if it had been there for half a century or more. The air was filled with an ancient sulfurous stench tinged more recently with sewage. Annja had to take shallow breathes through her mouth. When she reached the bottom of the ladder, she stepped away from it in the darkness and flipped on her helmet light.

She was standing in a brick-lined sewer tunnel. It was dry, indicating it hadn't been used in many years, and extended in both directions as far as she could see.

Gianni stepped down off the ladder and took a moment to turn on his own headlamp, as well. Above, they heard a scraping sound as Vladimir replaced the ventilation grate. He then joined them at the bottom of the ladder.

"This way," he said, setting off.

Vlad kept to the center of the tunnel, his lamp lighting the way ahead. They hadn't gone very far before they began to see evidence that the tunnels weren't deserted. Discarded trash, sleeping areas made of cardboard and cast-off clothing, occasional piles of human waste.

"Gypsies, criminals, political refugees, ex-soldiers, the mentally ill—the underground is haven to them all," Vlad explained. "Entire communities have moved down here to escape the rat race up above. And, of course, those who like to prey on such people have found their way down below, as well."

Annja had been in places far more dangerous than this, but something about the darkness of the tunnels and the knowledge that there might be people out there watching them under cover of that darkness made her uneasy. She kept her right hand free, just in case she needed to call her sword in a hurry.

It wasn't long after Vlad had answered Annja's unspoken question that they had their first encounter with Moscow's underworld. They had been making their way down a rounded six-foot-wide tunnel that reminded Annja of a giant aqueduct when they turned a corner and were suddenly in the middle of a homeless encampment.

People lined either side of the hall—some standing, some sitting, some curled up in blankets and trying to get some sleep. The lights of a cooking fire or a Bunsen burner broke the darkness here and there, causing shadows to dance and sway along the walls like a crowd of ghosts watching them pass.

Vlad didn't stop or acknowledge the presence of the people in the tunnel in any way. He just kept moving, so Gianni and Annja had no choice but to follow.

It was the silence that bothered Annja the most. No one moved; no one said a word. With that many people in a confined area there should have been background noise—coughing, shifting of positions, talking—but this group was so quiet, Annja could hear each step that the three of them made. It was downright eerie and the feeling of being watched took a long time to leave her.

They made several turns, descended two more ladders, advanced another few hundred feet and then came to a halt. Glancing past Vlad, Annja could see the tunnel ahead was blocked by a giant turbine, its three-foot-long blades menacing despite the thick layer of dirt and dust that showed how long it had been since the blades were operational.

"Now what?" Gianni asked, clearly not relishing the idea of retracing their steps to find a different route.

Vlad's only answer was to put both hands on the center portion between the blades, and push. The entire turbine assembly swung outward on noisy hinges. With a glance at Gianni and a half-hidden smirk, Vlad waved them through the opening. Once they were on the other side, Vlad pushed the turbine back into place with the same noisy shriek.

"Ten-minute rest, then we go on," he told them.

Annja sat with her back against the tunnel wall. She no longer felt ridiculous in the fireman's coat and rubber boots, especially given the amount of muck and sludge they'd had to move through to get this far. She unzipped her waist pack and pulled out a bottle of water and a granola bar.

Beside her, Gianni was doing the same.

"How much farther, do you think?" she asked Vlad.

"Twenty, maybe thirty minutes before we hit lower levels of the Kremlin. After that, it depends on how good is your map."

Fair enough.

When the break was over, they got under way, this time with Annja bringing up the rear. They left the wide tunnel behind and moved into a narrower one with long stretches of spaghetti-like green cables running along the ceiling. The cables were more modern-looking than anything they had seen so far, which gave Annja hope that they were getting closer.

A sound split the air somewhere in the darkness far behind her.

What was that?

She stopped and listened carefully.

At first, all she could hear was the tramp of the men's booted feet as they moved up the passage away from her.

She stood still, listening.

Then, after what felt like forever, it came again.

A muffled shriek.

She knew that sound.

Had heard it just a short while ago.

Someone had just pushed the turbine out of the way and was coming down the tunnel behind them.

19

It's one of the homeless people we saw earlier, Annja told herself. Probably looking for a place to bunk down for the night. Nothing to worry the others about.

As they continued, she kept an ear out for whoever it was behind them. After a while, Annja began to get the sensation that she was being watched. Again. It was like an itch in the center of her back that she couldn't scratch, but each time she turned around and shone her light in the tunnel behind her, she didn't see anything.

She didn't like it. If they were being followed, she wanted to know why. This creeping through the dark in their wake had to stop.

A few minutes later the tunnel bisected a natural cavern and Annja saw her chance. Several stalagmites rose toward the roof near the exit on the far side of the cavern. As the other two continued forward, Annja slid behind one close to the exit.

She switched off her light, summoned her sword and settled in to wait.

It didn't take long.

Just a moment or two after Vlad and Gianni had moved out of sight, Annja heard someone moving along stealthily behind them. She kept her back to the stalagmite she was hiding behind and held her sword in front of her with both hands. She held the blade perpendicular to the floor, edge downward, ready to swing it in a low, flat arc.

She could feel the intruder getting closer. Ten feet…eight…six…

She could hear the shuffle of booted feet against the earth floor.

Four feet…three…two…

Annja resettled her grip on the broadsword, took a breath and then spun out of her hiding place, bringing the flat of the blade crashing into the head of their pursuer.

There was a sharp ringing sound as the blade struck something metallic, then the tinkle of broken glass followed by a stifled cry.

Now that she knew exactly where the intruder was, Annja didn't give him time to respond. She spun back the other way around the stalagmite and brought her blade flashing forward once again, this time smacking it against the back of her opponent's knees, knocking his legs out from under him and leaving him flat on his back before he even knew what was happening.

She knelt on his chest and with her free hand flipped the lamp of her headlamp back on.

The light caught the newcomer in the face and shone directly into the night-vision goggles he wore. The man uttered a shriek and tore the goggles off to keep himself from being blinded by the magnified light.

He wore civilian clothing and a good pair of hiking boots. But he was either government or military. Somehow she just knew it.

While he was still dazed, Annja hauled him to his feet and slammed him against the cavern wall. She pressed the edge of her sword against his neck hard enough to draw a line of blood.

"Don't move or I'll slit your throat," she told him in a clear voice, so that he wouldn't misunderstand and try to escape. She didn't want to kill him but she would if he did something stupid.

She reached inside his coat and yanked a pistol out of the shoulder holster she found there. Realizing that her companions might come looking for her at any moment, she let the sword vanish back into the otherwhere and held the pistol on her captive instead. She dug around on the intruder's other side, finding a worn leather credentials case. A glance at the ID inside told her she was holding a member of the *Federal'naya sluzhba bezopasnosti,* or Federal Security Service.

Always a nice way to spend an afternoon.

She took a step back, keeping the gun out but not pointing it directly at him.

"Who are you and why are you following us?" she asked him.

He answered her in Russian.

She didn't understand the words but she got the gist. *Sorry, don't speak English.*

She brought the gun up and pointed it in his face. "Cut the crap. I know you understand me perfectly. All FSS agents are required to speak and understand English."

It was a total bluff. She had no idea what the language requirements were for being an agent but she figured it was worth a shot.

To her surprise, it worked.

"I am just following orders," he said in accented English.

Before Annja could say anything further, she heard Vlad and Gianni calling her name.

"Annja! Annja!"

"Over here!"

Seconds later the other two joined her in the cavern.

"Who the hell is that?" Gianni asked. She ignored him, focusing instead on the Russian.

"What orders? Who told you to follow us? And what were you supposed to do when you caught up?"

"I was supposed—"

That was as far as he got.

There was a crack of sound and almost simultaneously a bullet drilled itself through the face of the man she was holding captive, coming so close to Annja's own that she could feel the heat of its passage. Blood splattered all over her as the FSS officer's head disintegrated beneath the force of the impact.

For a moment, time stood still. Annja's thoughts whirled like a cyclone in her head.

What was he going to say that was worth killing him over? How many more were out there, in the dark, stalking them?

Then instinct took over and she was diving to the side, shouting, "Down!" and hoping like hell her companions were listening.

She hit the ground and rolled as bullets ricocheted off the rock wall where she'd been standing seconds before. She pulled herself around to the other side of a nearby stalagmite, hopefully out of the line of fire.

Shouts in Russian came from somewhere in the darkness, and then there was the sound of a shot from very close by.

Annja turned her head to see Vlad tucked as best he could behind another outcropping of stone, a big gun in hand. He sent another shot into the darkness, the report echoing loudly.

Just like that, the cavern was full of bullets flying everywhere. The enemy was on the far side of the cavern, firing from the cover of darkness, visible only when the muzzle flash lit the space around their guns. Annja had the dead FSS agent's pistol and was firing back, but more discriminately, waiting for those flashes of light, wishing all the while she hadn't accidentally smashed the FSS agent's night-vision goggles when she'd first struck him with her sword. Vlad produced another gun from somewhere on his person and was now alternating shots from one side of the pillar he hid behind to the other. Only Gianni was hanging back behind the protective cover of another stalagmite. And Annja couldn't blame him. He didn't have anything to shoot with and throwing rocks just really wasn't an option.

Their headlamps were making them perfect targets, but she didn't dare turn hers off. It would leave her effectively blind with no way to see if their enemies began to move up on them out of the darkness. Besides, if the rest of the invaders were wearing night-vision goggles like the first man had been, the light from the headlamps would actually be working against them, making it more difficult for their high-tech equipment to work.

The noise inside the room was deafening, the closeness of the chamber magnifying the boom of every shot tenfold, until Annja could barely hear anything but the gunfire.

It couldn't last long. She hadn't found any spare magazines when she'd quickly searched the now-dead Russian at her feet. Vlad might have an extra reload or two, but given the amount of bullets flying through the air, it wasn't going to be long before those, too, went dry.

She had to get them out of this before that happened.

Fate was conspiring against her, however.

Annja felt it first, a low rumbling vibration that seemed to come up from the soles of her feet. Small streams of dust and dirt began falling from somewhere above them and the stalagmite she was hiding behind began to move violently from side to side.

"Earthquake!" she heard Gianni shout.

It wasn't an earthquake, just a cave-in, but that didn't make it any less dangerous. Annja threw her hands up over her head to protect herself from falling debris. At a loud rumbling from behind her, she spun about, staring in amazement at what she saw.

A gaping hole was opening in the wall directly behind Gianni. Rocks and other debris tumbled outward, cascading down on her companion. One of those rocks struck him on the side of the head and he toppled over, clearly dazed.

The rapidly enlarging opening revealed another tunnel on the far side. With the intended route now blocked and their enemy preventing them from going back the way they had come, they didn't have much choice.

Down the rabbit hole it is, then.

Annja watched as Vlad stooped, grabbed the unconscious Gianni under both arms and dragged him through.

Afraid she'd be gunned down the moment she broke cover, Annja glanced back the other way, looking for some sign that the gunmen had beaten a hasty retreat of their own, but she couldn't see anything in the darkness.

Now or never, Annja.

"Come on!" Vlad shouted.

Eight steps. That's all it was between her and the tunnel where Vlad stood.

Eight steps.

She made four.

There was a thunderous crack from above as the roof of the cavern split open and then Annja was buried in what felt like a ton of earth and rock. Darkness enveloped her.

20

She regained consciousness with a heavy weight pressing against her. The ceiling collapse had dumped hundreds of pounds of earth, rock and ancient brick on her. Only her helmet had kept her alive, preventing her skull from being cracked open like an egg. She tried to move and discovered that she couldn't.

She couldn't move at all.

You're trapped.

You're going to die here.

Suffocate to death all alone.

"No, I will *not*," she said in fierce defiance.

She'd been trapped with her right arm thrust up over her head and her face tucked into the crook of her arm, creating a mini air pocket. That had kept her from suffocating.

Her head wasn't pounding the way she would have expected it to if she were upside down and all the blood was rushing to it, so she concluded she must still be facing upward, toward the surface.

If there even is a surface.

She was not going to give in to panic.

Her main problem was oxygen. Or lack thereof. That air pocket would be used up very quickly. The carbon dioxide she was emitting must already have significantly reduced the amount of oxygen in that tiny space. Her brain was starting to feel sluggish, her thought processes slowing down. If she didn't get more oxygen soon, she really would die here.

She couldn't move more than a few scant millimeters, certainly not enough to dig herself out. But then again, maybe she didn't have to.

Without moving a muscle, Annja reached into the otherwhere and drew her sword.

It sprang into existence, spearing upward from her outstretched hand and piercing the earth above her head. The tiniest whisper of air drifted down the length of her arm to reach her face.

It was musty and full of dirt particles, but it was air nonetheless.

There wouldn't have been enough light for her to see even if she hadn't been buried. But she could hear someone shouting and a strange rhythmic scratching sound. Like a giant cat scratching at the door to be let in.

Or someone digging into the earth nearby in an effort to rescue her.

"Here!" she shouted. "I'm here!"

She worked her wrist muscles, wobbling the blade in the channel it had created, sending earth cascading down toward her but widening the hole above her head, letting in more air. More sound.

Now she could make out the words.

"Hang on, Annja! We're coming!"

She could feel them now, somewhere down around her midsection. Their proximity made her realize she didn't need the sword anymore and being discovered with it would create its own host of problems. She let go of it and felt it vanish back into the nothingness of the otherwhere, ready for the next time she needed it.

That rhythmic scratching was much closer now, the sound filling her ears, and then she was being helped out of the mound of debris that had done its best to kill her.

She felt hands on her body, helping her sit up. There were lights in her face and cool water slipping past her lips. She spat to clear the dirt out of her mouth and then gulped it down, thankful to be alive.

"Easy," said Vladimir, and she looked up into his anxious face.

"What happened?" she asked, pushing the bottle of water away.

"All that gunfire brought the tunnel down on our heads."

"Gianni?"

"I'm good."

His voice had come from her left and with more effort than she expected—how long was I trapped in there, anyway?—she turned to get a look at him.

He'd seen better days, that was for sure. His face and hands were covered with dirt, though whether that was from being buried himself or the effort he'd expended to dig her free, she didn't know. But he smiled wearily and held up his hands in a "What are you gonna do?" gesture, so she knew he was all right.

"Did he say anything to you?" Gianni asked, and for a moment Annja didn't know what he was talking about.

He must have seen the confused look on her face. "The gunman," he explained. "Did the gunman say anything to you?"

Annja coughed, then spat some more dirt out of her mouth. She didn't want to scare either of them but they deserved the truth.

"They were federal agents. FSS. They were here under orders, but that's all I know."

Vlad swore loudly and rather vociferously in Russian. Or, at least, that's what Annja thought he was doing. She only recognized a word here or there, but that was enough to know he was not being very complimentary toward the Federal Security Service or those in its employ.

Gianni stared at her, an inscrutable expression on his face. "Is that all he said?"

"Yes. The truth was, he'd tried to say something more, but that's when a bullet took him." Another inch to the left and she would have been the one with the shattered face. She shivered to think about it.

Annja climbed to her feet and took a few tentative steps. When she didn't immediately collapse, she declared herself as good as new. She and the others then took stock of their situation.

The route they had previously been traveling was completely blocked by the cave-in. Which was a problem, because according to the map, the tunnel the FSS agents had rerouted them away from was the only one in this area that would lead them in the right direction. They were effectively cut off.

Even worse, they were now in unfamiliar territory in this newly revealed tunnel. To get out, they were going to have to explore virgin territory and hope for the best.

Great, Annja thought. Just great.

At least they still had the map. Not the original; that was safely back at Vlad's flat. The one she was carrying was a hand-drawn copy. She dug it out of the pocket of her pants and passed it over to Vlad, who took it with a nod.

Now came the hard part.

They set off down the tunnel before them with Vlad in the lead. Gianni's headlamp had been damaged in the collapse, so he was in the middle, leaving her to bring up the rear.

The tunnels here were smaller and, from the looks of them, considerably older. The brick-lined passageways were gone, leaving earthen walls shorn up with thick beams and the occasional section of tunnel that had been bored through solid rock. Unlike many they had passed through earlier, there was very little evidence of recent human occupation. No tracks through the dust, no discarded trash, no piles of human waste.

Vlad followed some internal compass known only to him. Whenever there was a fork in the passageway, he would stand before the two choices for a moment, considering, and then make a decision based on some hidden criteria Annja couldn't figure out. Each decision was made without hesitation, however, and it was for that reason Annja kept plodding along in his wake. She'd trusted him before and saw no reason not to continue doing so at this point. If anyone was going to get them out, it would be Vlad.

As if in answer to her confidence, about two hours after they had set off from the cave-in, a horrendous stench filtered down to them from the tunnel ahead. It was so horrible Annja found herself gagging, trying to bring the air back up out of her lungs.

Vlad, on the other hand, smiled.

"Yes! Most excellent!"

Most excellent? Annja thought. Are you insane?

She understood what he meant, however, when they'd progressed through a few curves and were abruptly stopped by a river of black goo that tried to grip their boots. The source of the horrible stench. The black substance was emanating from a vertical shaft that opened into the center of the passageway. Vlad marched over to it, his boots making a loud sucking sound every time he lifted a foot.

"Come," he said to them cheerfully. "Look." He pointed up the shaft.

Reluctantly Annja made her way over to his side. Looking up she was surprised to see light and the plastic edge of a toilet seat high above.

"Hotel Homeless," Vlad explained. "Height of European poshness."

Annja couldn't tell if that last was said in sarcasm or not. She also found herself wondering what the guests of the hotel would think about the way their waste was being disposed.

"Not much farther."

Vlad was right. Ten minutes later they climbed another set of ladders similar to those they'd descended to enter the underground. The grate at the top lifted easily in Vlad's big hands and they crawled out into street in front of the Hotel Homeless itself. An encampment at the edge of the city that was home to those who were down and out.

Moments later Vlad was on his cell phone, making contact with the comrade who had picked up the van.

They had survived their first journey into the Moscow underground.

21

The rendezvous point was an abandoned military warehousing facility that had been mothballed shortly after the end of the Cold War. It was about a twenty-minute drive from the Kremlin. Goshenko's driver was waiting for him beside a black Mercedes with government plates when Goshenko emerged from the building with Sergeant Danislov in tow. The two men climbed into the back and a moment later the driver pulled into traffic with all the grace of a barracuda slicing into a school of fish. Goshenko sat in icy silence, furious that such a simple plan had gone so awry. The coded message had been sent to Danislov fifteen minutes before.

Target acquisition lost due to tunnel collapse. Crew injured. Awaiting new instructions at rendezvous point Charlie.

It was a complete disaster and one that didn't bode well for Goshenko's search for the library. Without Creed and the map she had taken from the hand of the Virgin in Saint Basil's, his chance of finding the vault where Ivan's books were hidden was considerably lessened.

"Explain this to me," the colonel snapped.

Danislov made no excuses as he laid out what had happened in crisp, clear sentences. "I divided my men into five-man teams and assigned them locations throughout the city where the fugitives might try to reach. One of those positions was an old ventilation shaft near Moscow University, used by many of the region's homeless to access the underground."

With the smallest of hesitations, he continued. "My intent had been to join whichever team encountered our fugitives first and to take command myself. But my man on the ground took that option out of my hands when he chose to follow Miss Creed and her companions when they entered the tunnels."

"Why didn't he wait?"

"My guess is that he was concerned he would lose them in the tunnels. By the time I arrived at the location he'd reported in from, both Creed and my team were long gone. I descended into the tunnels, but with no idea which direction they had gone or the equipment I would need to navigate underground, I had no choice but to retreat."

"You guess?"

"Yes, sir. I haven't had the chance to speak to the man personally yet, so all of this is conjecture on my part."

"And you don't know what happened after that?"

Danislov shook his head. "No, sir. The unit's radio equipment failed almost immediately after they entered the underground. I received their coded message only moments before I relayed it to you, after they had emerged from the underground."

Goshenko cursed beneath his breath.

The gates were open when they arrived and the driver went through, pulling to a stop a few hundred yards farther down the road in front of a long warehouse. Colonel Goshenko got out of the vehicle almost before it had come to a complete stop and Sergeant Danislov scrambled to follow.

Five men had followed Miss Creed and her companions into the underground. Now only three remained—the squad leader, Chernov, and two others—and they looked like hell. All three had minor injuries and at least one of them had a pressure bandage wrapped around his head, indicative of a more serious problem. They were covered in grime and other less identifiable substances which, from the smell of them, were probably best left unmentioned. The corpse of a fourth man lay stretched out on the floor, not far from where the unit commander was standing.

Goshenko barely spared the others a glance as he

marched over to the group's leader, a man named Nikolai Chernov.

"What happened?" Goshenko demanded.

Chernov explained that they'd been casing the entrance to the underground as ordered when the woman and her two companions had suddenly emerged from a van close to the grate. The trio had spent several minutes gearing up before removing the steel grate, and disappearing into the tunnels right before their eyes.

"I didn't want to lose them the way the first team had at the hotel, so I made the decision to enter the tunnels and pursue them as closely as I dared."

Of course they'd followed Creed and her companions. What else could they have done given their orders to find and detain them? Goshenko nodded, impatient to get to the important part of the story.

They had lost radio contact with Sergeant Danislov shortly after entering the tunnels and so he'd been unable to keep them abreast of what was happening. That didn't make him any less culpable for what happened next as far as the colonel was concerned. He'd had a mission to accomplish and he'd failed to carry it out. Goshenko was really just hearing him out to be certain there wasn't anything he had missed. He'd already made his mind up about the commander on the ride over.

According to Chernov, he and his men had followed Creed and her companions deeper into the tunnels, going down several levels until they reached an older section of the underground. Worried that his squad might be stranded in unfamiliar territory in darkness, he'd ordered his men to move in closer so they didn't risk losing their quarry.

Somehow, the woman had become aware of their presence and laid an ambush for their point man.

"An unarmed woman ambushed a fully armed FSS officer?" Goshenko asked, his voice dripping with disbelief.

"Yes, sir. She wasn't unarmed, though, sir."

Finally, a new piece of information, Goshenko thought. "So she fired on your man?"

Chernov winced. "No, sir. Not exactly."

"What, exactly, happened, then, if she didn't fire upon him?"

"She attacked him with a sword, sir."

Goshenko stared at him.

"A sword?"

"Yes, sir. She must have surprised him in the darkness and used the sword to take him captive. He was scouting ahead and when I caught up with him, the woman was standing with her weapon to his throat. From my position I could hear her asking him questions."

"I…see. A sword. Really."

Goshenko shot a look over at Danislov, but the other man remained quiet. Turning back to Chernov, the colonel said, "Go on."

"She took his weapon from him and then used that to hold him captive."

"What happened to the sword?"

"It, uh, vanished, sir."

"Vanished?"

Realizing how that sounded, Chernov tried to temper his statement. "She must have put it down once she had the gun, sir. I didn't see it anymore, at least."

"Uh-huh. Go on."

To keep his subordinate from talking to their target, Chernov had been forced to terminate the other man. The target had begun firing back down the tunnel in their direction as a result, causing the other men in the unit to respond in kind. All that gunfire caused the already-unstable tunnel to collapse, burying the target and her companions beneath the deluge.

"We barely escaped with our lives," Chernov concluded.

Goshenko didn't care how close they'd come to dying. That was what he paid them for—to take risks. What he cared about was Annja Creed.

"Where is the body?" he asked, looking around the room for it, determined to find something worth salvaging. Maybe she'd written her thoughts down in a notebook or on a scrap of paper....

"Body, sir?"

"Yes, the body. Creed's body. Where did you put it?"

"Uh, we didn't recover the body, sir."

Goshenko rounded on the other man. "What?"

"We didn't recover the body, sir."

"You left Annja Creed's body in the tunnels?" the FSB colonel asked in an icily calm voice, pinning the man in place with his stare like a bug on a specimen board.

Several feet away, Danislov stood, watching, silent. A drop of sweat slipped down the side of Chernov's face.

"It was buried under an avalanche. What were we supposed to do, sir?"

Goshenko had to give him credit, this Chernov had done a decent job of relaying only the facts in the face of his own obvious animosity and might have managed to get out of there with more than his rank intact if he'd stuck to doing so. But responding with a question of his own, even a rhetorical one, had pushed a dangerous man's button.

Goshenko didn't leave any time for the question to settle. It was still there, floating in the air before them, when the colonel said quietly, "Sergeant."

Danislov stepped forward and snapped to attention beside Goshenko.

"Sir."

The colonel ignored the salute, snatching the pistol from Danislov's belt. He pointed the gun at Chernov's face and pulled the trigger.

A bullet hole appeared in the middle of the team

leader's forehead. Blood, bone and brain matter splashed on the wall behind him as the bullet exited the back of Chernov's skull. He hit the ground like a two-hundred-pound bag of wet sand.

The gunshot echoed in the abandoned warehouse for a moment and then faded away. Into the silence that followed, Goshenko said to Danislov, "I want that body found and brought back to the surface. I don't care if you have to excavate half of Moscow to do it."

"Understood."

Without another word, he turned and strode out of the warehouse.

22

The next morning the three of them sat around Vlad's tiny apartment in uncomfortable silence. No one wanted to be the first to suggest that their expedition was over, but it was certainly looking that way. The cave-in had been bad and they were lucky to have escaped unscathed. Annja had a newfound appreciation for Vlad's ability to navigate underground. Without him they would probably still be wandering those endless tunnels, lost in the dark.

Her thoughts turned to their assailants from the night before. Had they really been FSS agents? If so, what had they wanted?

From Annja's perspective, there seemed little chance the armed men had stumbled on her and her companions by accident. She had seen a spark of recognition in the first man's eyes when she'd confronted him. He'd clearly known who she was and had been about to say something directly to her when he'd been gunned down in cold blood. She was regretting not having had the chance to search him for anything that might have helped her ascertain that he was who his ID said he was.

Someone who was a little bit paranoid might think that the men they'd encountered in the tunnels were after the same thing they were—the library. Or, at the very least, what Annja and her team knew about the library's whereabouts. Someone who was very paranoid might even come to the conclusion they'd been there to capture or kill one of them. Annja was convinced it was all of the above.

She glanced over at Gianni but couldn't quite see him as a target of a Russian hit squad. The same went for Vlad; he might be loud about certain issues, but she couldn't imagine any of his rhetoric bringing down the wrath of the FSS.

Which left only Annja.

She'd been racking up quite an impressive list of enemies, as her quest had put her in the crosshairs of several criminals, from petty thieves to international terrorists. Just about all of them—the ones who were still alive—had reason to want her dead, and what better place to arrange for her to have an "accident" but deep beneath a city far from home?

It wasn't a comforting thought.

Then again, if she wanted comfort, she would have stayed at home.

Tired of the silence, Annja asked, "Well, now what?"

That got Gianni's attention, at least.

"Now what?" he repeated, incredulous. "Now we're done. Or did you happen to miss the four tons of rock that just cut off the only route we have?"

Annja cut him some slack and bit back the retort that sprung to mind. He was upset; they all were. But she wasn't the type to give up after a single try and there was no way she was going to throw up her hands and call it quits that easily.

As she opened her mouth to say so, Vladimir spoke up from the other side of the room. "*Nyet*," he said in that deep rumbling voice of his. "We are not done. There is more than one way to, how you say, make cat skinless?"

"To skin a cat," Annja corrected automatically. "You know another route, don't you?"

He shrugged. "Is possible. Not sure yet. Let me see map."

Annja glanced over at Gianni, who thought it over for a moment and then handed over the map they'd found hidden in the Virgin's hand.

Vladimir unfolded it and laid it out on the kitchen table. He studied it for a long moment, grunted to himself and then disappeared into a back room. He returned a moment later with an old-fashioned ledger book, which he put on the table next to the map.

As he flipped through the ledger, Annja could see

that the pages, like the walls in the front room, were covered with inked drawings of subterranean tunnels. Each drawing had been annotated by hand in fine Cyrillic script. It hit her then that what Vladimir had here was a treasure in and of itself, a constantly updated catalog of all he had seen and done in the caverns and tunnels beneath the city.

Annja's hopes rose. Without the maps the task had seemed hopeless. It would have taken them years to figure out a way around the collapsed tunnel and to get them back on track. But now, with the information Vlad had so carefully collected over the years, it might actually be possible....

Their host spent several minutes comparing the images on various pages of his ledger to the map on the table in front of him. At last, he sat back with a satisfied expression.

"Yes. It is possible. Very difficult, but possible."

Annja liked the "possible" part. "Talk to me, Vlad."

"We will have to go much deeper—six, maybe seven levels down. We intersect original tunnel here," he said, pointing to a spot on the map on the other side of the cave-in.

Gianni joined them at the table. "If we've still got a chance at going after the library, what are we doing sitting around here, then?"

"Not so easy," Vlad replied, shaking his head. "This route much more dangerous."

"How so?" Annja asked. They'd already survived a tunnel collapse and an attack by what she suspected was a Russian hit squad. She didn't see how it could get much more dangerous.

Vladimir pulled two folded sheets of paper out of the back of his ledger. When he opened the first, the others could see that it was a modern map of the Moscow subway system. He pointed to an area marked as the Ramenskoye District, about fifty kilometers from the city center.

"Just after World War II, Stalin built underground city here in Ramenskoye."

"An underground *city?*" Gianni echoed.

"*Da,* city. Built to hold up to 15,000 people." Vlad drew a finger across the map to show where it stretched. "From here…to here. To protect senior staff and their families in case of war with the West."

"What happened to it?" Annja asked, even though she suspected she already knew.

Vladimir shrugged, then confirmed her suspicions. "Nothing. The bunker is still there."

Gianni looked confused. "Can someone tell me why we're talking about a bunker complex? The library is somewhere beneath the Kremlin, not halfway across Russia in some underground fallout shelter, for heaven's sake."

The big Russian turned to answer, but Annja beat him to it.

"Metro-2," she said in a voice filled with disbelief.

She'd certainly heard of it; given *Chasing History's Monsters'* penchant for urban legends, how could she not? But she'd always assumed that this was really nothing more than fanciful rumor.

That rumor claimed that there was a second, secret subway system that paralleled the public metro system, designed and built by the government for use in the event of an emergency. The KGB was supposed to have built the first line on Stalin's behalf, running directly from the Kremlin to the Soviet leader's private dacha. Several other lines were rumored to run between various ministry buildings and bunkers like the one beneath Ramenskoye.

Of course, that's all they were, rumors, right?

"Da," Vlad said, dispelling that notion like a will-o'-the-wisp, "Metro-2." He unfolded the second piece of paper. This was a map, as well, but unlike the first it had been hand-drawn on very thin paper. A moment later she understood when Vlad laid it over the subway map, allowing the first map to show through the second and revealing how the Metro-2 tunnels crisscrossed those of the more modern Moscow metro.

"We enter through Ramenskoye bunker, here," Vlad said, pointing to a shaded area on the handdrawn overlay. He then traced a blue line that ran across the city to another shaded area. "Take this tunnel here until we reach Academy of Oceanology warehouse. Use Kremlin tunnel system from there to reach vault."

Annja studied the map, trying to get a sense of the plan's viability. It was difficult, given the vague details and the fact that she didn't understand the language well enough to make heads or tails of the annotations.

"Have you taken this route before?" she asked.

Vlad hesitated. "No," he said. "Map comes from a trustworthy source, but is not mine. Am confident I get you in and out without difficulty."

It wasn't the answer she was hoping to hear, but it would have to do. After all, what choice did they have? Give up the hunt? Not a chance, not after what they'd been through already. She was just going to have to trust him. He'd gotten them out of one scrape already.

"All right," she said, looking up at them. "Let's do this."

THE CALL CAME IN AROUND ten o'clock that morning. Goshenko was in the office and happened to pick up the phone himself, rather than waiting for his secretary to get it.

"Good morning, Colonel."

It was a man's voice, though not one he recognized. Which was unusual, as there weren't many people outside the FSS who had this number. The caller spoke in Russian, but Goshenko thought he could detect a slight accent behind the words, marking whoever it was as a nonnative.

"Who is this?"

"That's not important. What *is* important is that we are both searching for the library."

Goshenko didn't see any advantage to playing coy, given that the caller had reached him on a private line.

"Go on," he said.

"I'd like to propose a partnership. I'll provide you with the information I have, including where and when that annoying television host is going to make another attempt to locate the library. And in exchange I receive a share of the treasure when the library is located."

"There won't be another attempt," Goshenko replied, his interest in the conversation rapidly dwindling. "Annja Creed is dead."

The momentary silence on the other end of the line was quickly replaced with laughter.

"I assure you, Miss Creed is quite well, despite the attempt your agents made to bury her alive."

Goshenko's attention was now fully on the caller. Only a handful of people knew he was interested in the library, and even fewer still were aware that he had men hunting for Annja Creed because of the map he suspected she had. Aside from Danislov, the only other men in on what had happened down there in the tunnels were even now boarding a plane to take them to their new tour of duty just north of the Arctic Circle. He'd signed the transfer paperwork immediately upon returning to his office. That left only two ways the caller could have come by his information. Either he had a mole very deep in Goshenko's organization or...

...he was working with Creed directly.

Colonel Goshenko suddenly had a very good idea just who his caller might be.

"When is this attempt supposed to take place?"

"Do we have a deal?"

"Yes. Provided your information checks out."

There was a moment of silence as his caller decided what Goshenko's word was worth. "Creed and her group will try again in a few hours. The starting point will be the bunker complex in Ramenskoye."

Ramenskoye?

"You can't be serious."

The caller ignored the comment. "They have a map, directing them to Fioravanti's vault. If we can get our hands on that, we won't need the Creed woman any longer."

23

As they piled into the van for the third time in less than seventy-two hours, Annja felt a decided sense of déjà vu. It seemed it was her destiny to drive around Moscow in a van that smelled like sewage, hunting for a library most of the world had forgotten existed.

You've come a long way, baby. She had to quash a sudden case of the giggles.

Thanks to heavy traffic, it took them just over an hour to get out of the city and then another forty-five minutes to reach Ramenskoye.

Annja felt pretty good. She'd expected to be exhausted after being buried alive the night before, but she'd awoken refreshed, although sore. It was something she'd noticed before because of the sword. Her body seemed to heal faster than normal. Her dexterity and reaction time were getting better, as well.

Gianni, on the other hand, wasn't doing so great. He was irritable, snapping at even the slightest of comments—a result, no doubt, of the pain he was feeling from the gash in the side of his head. Annja had cleaned the wound as best she could and wrapped it in gauze covered with a topical anesthetic, but that had probably worn off several hours ago.

Of the three of them, Vlad was the only one who had escaped without injury. His years of being in the underground had prepared him for the unexpected. Annja now understood why Sir Charles valued him so highly; Vlad was a good man to have around in a crisis.

While the big Russian drove, Gianni used the satellite phone to place a call to Charles Davies. It was just before dawn in Connecticut, but given that they were headed underground again and would be out of touch for some time after that, it was important to bring their benefactor up to speed on everything that had happened to date.

Or, rather, most of what had happened, she thought with a twinge of guilt.

She and Gianni had agreed between them that they would leave out any mention of the FSS hit squad, if, indeed, that had been what it was, and of Annja's own close call in the cave-in. Charles couldn't do anything about either event, and besides, they'd survived them, hadn't they?

Instead, they told him that the tunnel conditions had made it impossible to reach the vault from the direction they had originally planned on taking, so they were going to try an alternate route. He asked if they needed more equipment or more time to study the situation to be certain that the option they were choosing was the best one available, but they declined. They strongly suspected they weren't the only ones going after the library, and if they spent too much time thinking rather than doing, they might miss their chance entirely.

"All right, Annja," Charles said, "I'll trust your judgment. That's why I hired you, to make decisions and run the expedition the way you see fit. But if things get difficult, I want you to pull back and rethink this."

Does infiltrating a hidden Soviet bunker to ride on a subway train that may or may not actually exist count as difficult? she wanted to ask. And to think some people didn't see restraint as one of her finer qualities.

"I will," she said, and then made arrangements to check in with him again inside of the next forty-eight hours.

Annja handed the phone back to Gianni, who slipped it into his pocket.

Not long after the conversation with Sir Charles Davies, Vlad left the main road behind for a little-used forest road about eight kilometers outside of Ramenskoye. They climbed steadily as they drove deeper into the forest, advancing for another couple of miles before Vlad pulled the car into the lie of a large pine and parked.

"Walk from here," Vlad told them.

They gathered their gear from the back of the van, double-checked that their lights worked and that they all had extra light sticks and water bottles in their pockets and then set off once more. This time moving northward through the trees.

Ten minutes later they found themselves standing before a heavy chain-link fence. A sign hanging on it no doubt warned of all the terrible things that would happen to them if they were caught trespassing in the compound on the other side, but since she couldn't read it, Annja didn't feel as if she was breaking any rules by ignoring it. While some of the lettering was faded from long exposure to the elements, the red hammer and sickle emblem still stood out starkly against the white background.

While Annja and Gianni watched, Vlad used bolt cutters to cut a rectangular opening into the fence, which when viewed sideways looked like a U with the opening to the left. He then peeled back the loose section, holding it open for them to slip through before following. Once he was on the other side, he let the loose section of the fence fall back into place and then secured it with a couple of plastic zip ties.

It wouldn't pass close inspection, Annja knew, but from a distance it would help make the fence look as if it was still intact and hadn't been tampered with.

The fact that Vlad went to such trouble to hide their presence out here in the middle of nowhere either spoke to the care he took with every task or the fact that this area might still be in use by active military personnel, despite the Red Army's sigil on that sign.

Annja really hoped it was the former.

Without a word Vlad set off again, cutting through the trees on a slightly eastern heading this time. The woods around them were quiet, the only sounds the tramp of their feet through the undergrowth and the occasional snap as a branch broke beneath their weight. After another ten minutes, they reached their destination.

In the valley below them was the Soviet-era facility Vlad had told them about. It might have looked like the campus of a small, private college in Anywhere, U.S.A., if the college had chosen to construct its buildings from thick gray stone and undecorated steel. The buildings gave off a distinct sense of menace, as if the nature of the work that had gone on there imparted a certain personality that lingered like a ghost.

Annja didn't like the look of the place.

She wasn't alone in her reservations, either. Gianni hung back, not wanting to go too deep into the compound, it seemed; he kept glancing behind them as if expecting someone to be there.

Vlad, however, barely noticed their anxiety, or if he did notice he pretended not to. He led them across the campus until they reached a small, unassuming building off the beaten path from the rest of the compound. He produced a key and unlocked the door. Taking them down several hallways, only their booted feet broke the silence, a silence that felt as if it had fallen over the place centuries ago. Annja was starting to second-guess the whole idea of coming here in the first place when Vlad stopped so abruptly she almost walked into him.

"We are here," the big Russian said, and Annja looked around at the empty hallway and the door at the far end. What on earth was Vlad talking about? There wasn't anything here.

Gianni voiced what she was thinking.

"We're here?" he asked, the sarcasm in his voice loud and clear. "Where, exactly, is 'here' and what are we supposed to do from this point?"

By way of reply, Vlad walked over to the door, opened it and shone his light down the stairwell on the other side, leading deeper into the earth. He turned toward them and smiled that trademark smile of his.

"The underground awaits, my friends."

24

Sergeant Danislov watched on the closed-circuit camera as Miss Creed and her two companions descended the stairs and began the long walk down the hall toward the exit at the other end. Occasionally Annja would peer in through a window or try a door, but they were always locked. This wasn't surprising to Danislov, for he'd gone down that same hallway not twenty minutes before and locked them all himself. He didn't want Miss Creed and her companions straying from the carefully chosen script he'd decided they should follow.

Two hours ago Colonel Goshenko had called him into his office and handed him the plans for this Soviet-Army-base-turned-KGB-training-facility.

"Creed survived," Goshenko had said bluntly.

The surprise must have shown on Danislov's face, because Goshenko had added, "Yeah, I felt the same way. Should have known Chernov was an idiot the minute he started talking about that sword. My only regret is that I didn't shoot him early enough."

"Where is she now?" Danislov had asked.

"Making another attempt to reach the library through the mothballed facility for which I just handed you the blueprints. I want you to be sure she succeeds."

It was perhaps the last thing Danislov had expected to hear and for a moment he'd been at a loss for words.

The colonel had grinned. "Ask yourself this— why should we go through all the tedium of looking for Ivan's vault ourselves when we can just let Creed do all the work and then take what's ours once the work is done?"

Now Danislov watched them move deeper into the facility. "Keep going," he murmured, "keep going."

The plan was a simple one. He was going to drive Creed forward, little by little, step by step, until she brought them to the vault's doorstep.

And after that, well, Miss Creed wouldn't be important anymore, would she?

The first order of business, it seemed, was getting them into the next section of the base.

THEY DESCENDED THIRTEEN stories—Annja kept track of each pair of landings they passed, counting them off in her head, noting the number—until they reached the bottom floor. The lights on their helmets stretched out along the corridor that opened up before them, revealing the stark design and lack of aesthetics that had been de rigueur in the height of the Soviet era.

Vlad reached over and flipped a switch on the wall.

Lights came on along the ceiling.

"How'd you do that?" Annja asked. If the base hadn't been used in years, the electricity shouldn't still be running, should it?

"Reactor built first in early 1980s. Big enough to power entire city. Ramenskoye built after that, directly on reactor. Base probably still have working light long after rest of us are dead."

A Soviet reactor running quietly without supervision somewhere beneath their feet. Running for the past thirty years. The hair on her arms stood up. What if the wall of that reactor had been decaying all this time, letting the poison that powered it seep out into the earth around them? How would anyone know what was going on if the facility wasn't monitored regularly?

They wouldn't, she realized, and that was not a comforting thought.

They followed those lights down the corridor for what felt like forever. Only occasionally would the monotony of the bare walls be broken by the sudden appearance of a door, but each time Vlad passed it, intent on some other destination. Annja couldn't resist trying a few of the doors they passed along the way. They were always locked, though, so she stopped bothering.

Eventually the corridor ended at a door exactly like all the other doors they had passed.

"What's behind this one? More stairs?" Annja teased, but Vlad shook his head.

"No stairs," he said. "Something much more amazing."

He opened the door and gestured for them to go ahead.

Stepping through, Annja processed how enormous the space was. She couldn't see far with her light, but she could feel the emptiness, the way you could when you stood on the end zone in an indoor football stadium and stared down the length of the field toward the other end.

Vlad moved to the wall, opened up a control panel that reminded her of an old-fashioned fuse box and began to throw switches.

Out in the darkness, lights began to come on. They were so artfully arranged that because of the use of angles and mirrors you didn't see any single lamp. The effect was that of all the lights combined into one large lamp, like a sunrise.

The first thing she noticed after that was the Golden Arches. They were so incongruous that she actually rubbed her eyes. But they were there all right, on a street that looked as if it had been taken directly out of small-town America.

From where she stood she could see a Mercantile Bank, an Ace Hardware store, a 7-Eleven, a Sunoco gas station, a Stop & Shop grocery store...a public park and an elementary school. What looked to be a couple of blocks of residential dwellings spread out in both directions from the town center, as if in replica of the way small communities all across America had sprung up around a central common and expanded outward from that point.

"What on earth?" Gianni began, and then lapsed into muttered Italian as he struggled to figure out just what it was he was looking at.

Annja knew exactly how he felt. What was small-town America doing deep beneath a Soviet military base in the middle of nowhere?

Then it hit her.

She was looking at a "charm school," a KGB training facility designed to teach Soviet sleeper agents how to act like Americans before sending them to become part of American society.

She turned and looked at Vlad in astonishment.

"Is this what I think it is?" she asked.

"Da," Vlad said. "Soviet spies trained here to be Americans. Order Mickey D's hamburgers, save money in bank account, shop at grocery store. Just like you."

Actually, Annja couldn't remember the last time

she'd done any of those things—she ordered out far
more often than she cooked anything for herself,
never mind shopped at a grocery store—but she
knew what he meant.

Vlad pointed to the far end of the stadium-like
space, where it looked like the miniaturized forms
of skyscrapers were rising up over a faux city.

"Metro station that way," he said. "Tunnel will
take us direct to Kremlin."

Annja made note of its location. It would be a
good rendezvous point if they got separated.

They set off down the main road and Annja marveled at the details, from the fire hydrants and white
picket fences along the street to the old-fashioned
cars parked at the curbs. She couldn't help but go into
the bank for a few moments. It was like something
out of an old eighties cop show, with open teller windows instead of massive sheets of bulletproof glass.
A sign inside talked about mortgage rates just above
nine percent and Annja blinked at that. She didn't
remember times being that bad, but then again, she'd
only been a child in the eighties.

Seeing Happy Meals listed for two dollars and
apple pies for fifty cents was like going back to
a time she barely remembered, where a family of
four could eat for less than ten bucks and the sign
out front under the Golden Arches read 80 Billion
Served.

They'd gotten so much right—the width of the

sidewalks, the height of the picket fences, the size and shape of the fire hydrants. It was incredible and she could imagine what it had been like when it was operational, full of people pretending to be Americans every minute of every day.

They were halfway across the training ground when the lights went out.

The sudden darkness brought Annja up short and she let out a whispered, "You've got to be kidding!" It was blacker than black all about her, a darkness so complete that it felt as if it had substance and weight all its own.

Annja didn't like it.

Which was why she was quite happy to see some small lights come on throughout the "town" a moment later. Streetlamps, lights behind the windows of the residences, small pinpoints of light in the "sky" above simulating stars. It was like standing outside in those moments right after the sun had set and night had fallen.

Vlad happened to be standing near a streetlamp and as its light fell on his face she could see that he was worried.

"What is it?" she asked.

Vlad frowned, then pointed a finger skyward. "Lights on timer. Sun sets six hours after system starts."

"Which means what, exactly?" Gianni asked, his

eyes narrowing as he pondered the implications of Vlad's statement. "Is it a malfunction of some kind?"

Vlad shrugged. "Maybe."

That seemed to satisfy Gianni, but not Annja. She'd heard the doubt in Vlad's voice and wasn't yet ready to let the matter go.

"If it's not a malfunction, what else could it be?" she asked, knowing the answer but wanting to hear him say it, anyway.

He looked right at her, letting her see the concern in his own eyes as he said, "Someone resetting system manually."

Annja liked that idea even less. They were deep underground in a long-abandoned military facility that your average Russian probably didn't even know existed, never mind knew how to find. No way was someone just going to stumble on the place at the exact same moment they were passing through it.

That could mean somebody else was here specifically because the three of them were, which made her think of the squad in the tunnels the night before. But why would they reset the system to this facility? What would it accomplish? And how had they found their trail so quickly? They must've arrived only moments apart. What did they want?

They wanted the map, of course. That was easy enough to figure out.

And she was the one holding it.

"Perhaps we'd better move a little quicker, just in case," she said, and Vlad agreed.

Annja happened to be looking over Vlad's shoulder when she said it and caught the gun flash. A moment later she felt the wind part her hair to the left of her face.

Then and only then did the rifle report reach them across the intervening space.

There was no time for subtleties.

"Run!" Annja yelled.

25

Annja broke left, instinctively heading down a side street that had its fair share of parked cars and over-hanging trees. She stuck to the dense shadows, not wanting to offer an easy target. Halfway down the street she cut left again, slipped between two houses and began working her way back in the direction they had come from, determined to catch a glimpse of whoever it was that kept interrupting their plans.

It didn't take long.

On the next street over she caught motion out of the corner of her eye and turned to see someone dash across the street and hunker down behind a nearby car.

She thought it might be Gianni. But she kept her mouth shut until she could get closer. If it was him, she didn't want to risk giving away their position.

She followed him, waiting to see what he would do.

It soon became clear that it wasn't Gianni at

all. For one thing the individual she was following seemed taller than the Italian. For another, his head looked oddly disfigured, pointed in the front and bulbous in the back, like it was swollen in all the wrong places.

So it wasn't Gianni and it wasn't Vlad, which meant he was a fair target.

She watched as the man hustled over to a new vantage point, hunkered down and then scanned the area. When she looked in the same direction he was looking, she couldn't see anything. The darkness swallowed up everything past the first five feet or so. That led her to the idea that her target could see better in the dark than she could.

That tidbit of information raised all sorts of interesting possibilities.

It was time she and the unknown individual she was following had a nice little chat.

She waited for him to move again, this time from behind a parked car to the edge of a house two yards over. As he got ready to check out the area directly in front of his hiding place, Annja rushed him on silent feet. As she got closer, she called her sword to her, reassured by its familiar weight when it appeared from the otherwhere.

Her target must have realized he was no longer alone and began to turn just as she swung the pommel of her sword into the side of his head.

She fully expected him to topple over unconscious, so she was caught by surprise when he reared up and grabbed her around the waist, lifting her off the ground as he got to his feet.

That's when she realized that part of the reason he'd looked so funny was his immense size; he had to be at least six and three-quarters, maybe even seven feet tall.

With her feet dangling in the air and her waist gripped tightly in her opponent's hands, Annja began to question the wisdom of her decision to chase him in the first place.

This close she could see that the bulbous thing she'd seen attached to the front of his head was a pair of military-issue night-vision goggles.

Her appreciation of the goggles he was wearing over his face came to an abrupt halt when he growled something at her in Russian and began to squeeze.

That's when she discovered that in addition to being freakishly tall, he also had hands like a vise. He had no intention of letting go and he let her know it by squeezing harder, laughing all the while.

Annja had had enough. Either this guy was a complete moron and didn't recognize the sword in her hands for what it was—how do you miss something like that?—or else he didn't think she would use it.

She fully intended to disabuse him of that notion in a very painful fashion.

But as she brought the sword up for that blow, she found that she couldn't do it. She couldn't kill him

like that. It just didn't seem fair. He was carrying a
pistol in the holster on his waist and he hadn't gone
for that when she'd come charging out of the darkness, had he? So how could she be so cavalier as to
thrust a sword through his heart?

Berating herself as an idiot, Annja reversed her
grip on the sword and brought the weapon's pommel slamming down on the top of the fool's head.

That was all it took. His limbs turned to rubber
and he went down.

Freed from his crushing grip, Annja took a couple of deep breaths to get the oxygen flowing and
reminded herself not to take on men twice her size.

After checking he'd be unconscious for some
time, Annja stripped him of the goggles. They looked
to be military-grade night-vision goggles, though
she'd be the first to admit that her experience with
them was limited. But she had had occasion to use
them before this and had at least a working knowledge of how they operated. She knew the long lens-
looking thing at the front gathered the ambient and
infrared light, then sent it inside the device where
some funky stuff with electrons and phosphors took
place, and then sent the image with its characteris-
tic green glow to the viewer. Either through the eye
cups on the device itself or to an external computer
monitor.

She brought the eye cups of the device up to her
face and looked through them.

The space around her swam into focus in brilliant green and she had no trouble seeing a good way into the distance.

Which was why she had no problem seeing the line of men advancing toward her through the darkness.

26

Annja immediately crouched along the side of the house, worried that if she could see them, they could probably see her. They were coming down the same street she, Gianni and Vlad had been on just moments before. They were armed and at least two of them looked to be carrying rifles or possibly shotguns in their hands in addition to the handguns.

Seeing that all of them were wearing the same type of goggles that she was now holding, she understood the reason they'd killed the lights. With the goggles, they had a distinct tactical advantage, never mind a psychological one, over Annja and her team.

She watched them for a moment, trying to gather as much information as she could in case any of it proved useful later. She hadn't seen the group that had attacked them in the tunnels the day before, but she suspected these were the same people. They looked fit and they moved with military precision, two things she wasn't happy to see. She would have bet her next paycheck that they were agents of the FSS.

Why the hell can't we shake these guys?

She stepped back around the side of the house, out of their line of sight, and took a minute to adjust the headgear. When she was finished she slipped it over her head and settled the goggles in place.

The guy she'd coldcocked still hadn't stirred so she bent and quickly searched him, pocketing the two spare magazines she found for his pistol as well as the handheld radio. A plan was forming in the back of her head, one in which she pushed back against those who had been pushing her for the past few days. And a little firepower was going to come in handy when it came time to carry out that plan.

She glanced around the corner to double-check the position of the other gunmen, then turned and headed in the other direction.

She needed to find the other two and let them know what was going on.

DANISLOV PUT THE RADIO to his lips and tried again. "Command to Subotin. Come in, Subotin."

Still no answer.

He'd sent the man out ahead to act as their spotter and to give them advance warning if Creed and her companions headed off in the wrong direction. Subotin had done well at first, letting Danislov know when Creed had wandered into the bank and then McDonald's. At one point he'd been so close he could have reached out and touched them; for all his size, Subotin could move swiftly and silently when he needed to. It was the reason Danislov had selected him for the duty in the first place.

Then, a few minutes ago, he'd gone silent and dropped off the air.

Danislov was growing worried. He'd seen how resourceful that Creed woman could be.

He cursed himself for taking that shot. It had seemed like a good idea at the time, the kind of thing to startle them into action, force them forward without giving them too much time to think. Leading him to the treasure without realizing they were doing so. Now, however, he thought it might have had the opposite effect, bringing Miss Creed's notoriously protective nature into the fray. Once riled, she rarely backed down, it seemed.

He brought the tracking device out of his pocket and glanced down at the tiny screen. It was blank, which told him the locator tab hadn't been activated yet.

That, at least, was effectively idiot-proof. The device went live the minute the backing was torn off the tab, so all their inside man needed to do was tear off the little slip of paper and slap the tab on whatever it was they needed to track.

In this case, one Annja Creed.

SHE STUMBLED ON GIANNI FIRST.

Annja had just cut through several yards, trying to get ahead of the FSS agents she'd seen approaching down the main avenue, when she spotted three men coming down a side street toward her.

There was a long wooden fence ahead of her, running parallel to the path the men were taking, and she ducked behind that

She found a spot where there was a reasonable gap between two of the fence slats, just enough room for her to observe the trio more closely. Something about the way the man in the middle moved reminded her of Gianni. Was he now a prisoner of the FSS? If that were the case, it wouldn't be long before all of their plans, and everything they knew to date about the library, were in the FSS hands. She didn't doubt for a second that they would be able to get him to talk.

She shifted position, trying to get a better look.

The trio walked beneath one of the streetlamps moments later and Annja had her confirmation.

It *was* Gianni.

He was walking with his head bowed, his hands out of sight within the depths of his jacket. Annja wondered if they were confined behind his back, but couldn't get a good enough view to know for sure.

On either side of him were armed FSS agents. One carried a rifle. The sight of the weapon sent Annja's blood to boiling; twice now someone had tried to kill her from a distance with a long-range rifle shot and she was growing tired of it.

It was time to teach someone a lesson.

Rescuing Gianni at the same time was an added bonus.

The fence ran perpendicular to the road for another thirty feet or so. She could see six, maybe eight cars—the angle made it hard to tell for sure—parked along the curb near the end of the fence. The one on the end was an oversize van.

Perfect...

She rose into a crouch and raced along the length of the fence, confident that it was high enough she wouldn't be seen. When she reached the end she double-checked to be sure she wouldn't be silhouetted by any lights at her back, and then cautiously peeked around the other side.

Gianni and his captors were just reaching the first of the cars at the back of the line opposite her. For the next moment or two Annja would be shielded from view by the bulk of the vehicles.

She dashed out from behind the fence and crouched next to the front tire on the passenger's side. She checked the gun in her hand, then leaned against the vehicle and waited.

She heard their voices first, a murmuring that carried in the still air. There was a quick sound of radio static, then a voice spoke out of the night, saying something over the airwaves in Russian. The men escorting Gianni laughed at whatever was said.

Come on…

Annja kept her head turned forward and her gaze focused on a spot about five feet past the front of the van. As soon as they passed into view…

Another voice spoke, this time a little louder, again in Russian.

Annja found that strange, because the voice had sounded an awful lot like Gianni's.

He doesn't speak Russian.

Then the first of his captors moved into view and Annja went into action.

"Don't move!" she said sharply, coming out from behind the van, swinging the barrel of the gun smoothly from one target to the other and back again. The night-vision goggles on her face allowing her to see them quite clearly even in the heavy shadows.

They abruptly did as they were told and stopped short.

The one on the far left started to move his right arm slightly and Annja took another step closer, the gun centering on his chest. "I said don't move. I'll put a bullet in your skull if you do it again."

She let some of her anger show in her voice, in case they didn't understand English. She didn't want there to be any confusion.

It was all unfolding as she'd planned, which was

why she should have known something would go wrong.

That something was Gianni.

"Annja? Is that you?" he asked, turning partially toward her and leaning forward. In doing so, for just a moment, his body blocked Annja's line of sight toward the FSS agent on her left.

It was what the gunman had been waiting for.

His left hand came up, the gun in it gleaming wickedly in the green light of the night-vision goggles.

If she wanted to live, Annja's only option was to pull the trigger and damn the consequences.

She did.

The gun in her hand went off with a shout and the bullet whipped past Gianni's cheek, missing him by a quarter of an inch. It punched a hole into the neck of the man behind Gianni, flinging him over backward with the force of the shot.

Her muscles kicked in even before her head had time to process what her instincts were telling her. She spun to the right and dropped to one knee as her opponent's finger tightened on the trigger. The rifle in his hands went off with a loud, flat crack.

There's no way he can miss at this range, Annja thought. And then he did just that, sending the bullet over her shoulder to disappear somewhere in the darkness behind her.

Annja fired back.

Unfortunately for him, she didn't miss.

When it was over, Gianni threw his arms around her in a hug. "Damn, but I thought I was a goner! Thanks for getting me out of that."

Annja shook her head. "We're not out of anything yet. The others are going to hear those shots and we need to be long gone by then. Come on!"

She ran to the nearest body and stripped the goggles off the man's head. Flipping them on, she handed them to Gianni and told him to hold them up in front of his face so he could see in the dark. They'd worry about proper fit later. For now, she just wanted an even playing field if they came up against any of the enemy.

Annja grabbed the rifle and headed down the nearest side street with Gianni in tow, wondering where on earth Vlad had gotten himself off to.

Let's hope he's waiting for us at the Metro-2 station, she thought.

27

The man in question was at that moment two hundred yards away and another twenty feet deeper underground, staring at the long silver train stretching out down the tracks in front of him.

The fabled Metro-2 tracks.

He almost couldn't believe it.

He'd been hearing about the existence of Stalin's secret subway system all his life, but not once in the past ten years he'd spent crawling in the mud, muck and mystery of the underground had he ever seen actual evidence that it was real. He'd found tracks, sure, but then again, who hadn't? But who had ever nailed down whether one set of tracks was a part of the mystery line or not?

Now, after all this time, he was staring at one of the very trains that Party officials had used to hide their comings and goings from the ministry buildings downtown to the secret facility above him.

He was almost giddy with excitement.

Until he remembered why he'd come down here in the first place.

He'd promised Annja he would get to her destination deep beneath the Kremlin and he fully intended to do that. He didn't care if the FSS was after her; he'd been wanted by the organization a time or two himself. Most of the members of the Urban Underworld had. For them, being hounded by the FSS, and before them the KGB, was a mark of status. It meant you were getting closer to the secrets they sought to keep buried. It meant you were having an impact.

Seems she's certainly doing that.

Which meant Vlad needed to keep up his end of the bargain if he was going to help her find Ivan's lost library.

The best way of doing that right now was to get this train running.

He glanced worriedly toward the stairs. Before someone had taken a shot at them out of the darkness, he'd shown Annja the Metro-2 station's location and he'd fully expected her to rendezvous with him here. Gianni, too. Except it had been at least ten minutes and neither of them had showed up yet. He was starting to think he needed to go back out and look for them.

That would mean the train wouldn't be ready to go when they needed it.

It was a tough call. In the end he decided he'd

give Annja another ten minutes. In the meantime, he could take a look at the train's control system.

The platform lights were on, giving him plenty of light to see by. The last engineer who'd driven the train had left it parked with the cab very close to the station platform. Vlad walked over and began to root around inside.

"I WANT YOU TO STAND right here and keep an eye out for any of those Russians," Annja told Gianni as she positioned him at the back of the hardware store where he would be partially hidden by a Dumpster. From his vantage point he'd be able to see out across the parking lot toward the main road.

They'd been headed for the far end of the training complex, the section that looked as if it had been designed to resemble a city and where Vlad had indicated they would find the Metro-2 station, when they'd passed the rear of the Ace Hardware store and Annja had gotten an idea.

"What are you going to be doing in the meantime?" he asked, even as he settled into place.

"I told you. I'm going to get us inside."

She went to the rear door and situated herself so that her back was to Gianni. She intended to break in and she didn't want him seeing her tool of choice.

They'd arrived to find the place locked up tighter than Fort Knox, both front and back. A thick iron chain had provided extra security to the front, but the owner had apparently decided that the rear door didn't need the same consideration. It was secured with a basic lock.

"What do we need from here, anyway?" Gianni asked.

"I want to leave a few presents for our Russian friends to remember us by."

"Presents from a hardware store?"

She glanced over at him, exasperated. "Just watch the street, will you?"

"Fine, fine, but don't blame me when…"

Annja tuned him out. Keeping her back to Gianni, she called her sword. One minute her hands were empty, the next they held a broadsword with a storied pedigree. She marveled at it for a moment, then turned and jammed the blade between the twin doors, right above the lock mechanism. She slid it in a few inches then brought it downward sharply.

The lock broke in two and the doors popped open.

Annja held her breath. If an alarm was going to go off, it would be now….

Nothing happened

She let the sword vanish before calling over her shoulder to Gianni. "I'll be out in a minute. If you see anyone, come get me."

"Get you. Right," he said from his vigil.

She slipped inside.

It took her a moment to orient herself, but once she had, she began to move briskly through the store, plucking what she needed off the shelves and stuffing it into a black nylon backpack she found hanging from a hook behind the cash register. She only needed a few items so it didn't take long.

When she came out the back door, Gianni was nowhere to be seen.

For a moment she panicked, convinced the Russians had waited until she was out of sight before snatching him right out from under her nose. Then he emerged from behind one of the parked cars at the back of the lot, self-consciously tugging up his zipper, and Annja had to suppress a laugh.

There was still no sign of their pursuers and that was starting to worry Annja. Had the FSS agents slipped ahead to cut them off from their destination, or had they pulled back to regroup now that she had shown she was a force to be reckoned with?

There was only one way to find out.

But first, she wanted to set up her surprise.

VLAD WAS KNEE-DEEP in the guts of the train's control panel when he heard it.

The scrape of boot leather on stone.

He picked up the heavy wrench he'd been using—the one he'd found along with the rest of the tools in a long-abandoned toolbox in the driver's compartment of the train—and prepared to defend his territory.

"Vladimir?"

His name was spoken barely above a whisper, but he recognized the voice.

"Over here," he said, leaning out of the cab to see Annja and Gianni standing on the platform.

Annja ran over and gave him a hug, which both surprised and pleased him. "How did you know it was me in there?" he asked.

Annja pointed over to where Vlad had left his trademark yellow fireman's jacket draped over the charging console.

Vlad grinned sheepishly.

Annja waved her hand in the train's direction. "Is that thing still running?"

"*Da.* Nuclear powered."

Annja blinked. "Come again?"

"The train. It's nuclear powered, like base above our heads. Will run for many years. Many, many years."

Gianni pointed at the cables running from the charging unit Vlad had dug out of a nearby equipment closet to the engineer's panel inside the conductor's car. "Then what's with the wires?"

"Secondary systems run on chargeable batteries. Charge was *nyet,* so I recharge."

Annja looked at the sixteen-car subway train with a sense of wonder that mirrored Vlad's reaction when he'd first seen it. "Will it take us where we need to go?" she asked.

"*Da.* Can leave in ten minutes, once charging complete."

Annja clapped him on the back. "Excellent! In the meantime, Gianni and I will set up a little surprise for our Russian friends."

He only hoped they had ten minutes to spare.

28

Danislov looked down at the dot glowing on the locator screen and allowed himself a smile. The tab had been activated a few minutes before and from there it was simplicity itself to follow it to the edge of the "city."

Based on the information the locator device was giving him, Creed and her companions had taken refuge in the Metro-2 station just ahead.

Danislov couldn't think of a better spot for them right now.

He glanced over at Subotin to his left. He'd found his former point man a few minutes ago, lying unconscious, his radio and weapons missing. No doubt they were now in the hands of the ever-resourceful Annja Creed.

Subotin wasn't happy. Being beaten by a woman in hand-to-hand combat had embarrassed him and he was itching for a chance to pay her back tenfold. This was a problem for Danislov, of course. He needed Creed whole and healthy, which was why Subotin was right here at his side where he could keep an eye on him.

Danislov picked up his radio and put the next phase of their operation into motion.

"Command to all units. Fugitives located in the Metro-2 station. Move in and secure."

He knew that Creed didn't speak Russian, but at least one member of her party certainly did. And he fully expected she had Subotin's radio.

When Vlad heard Danislov give the order for his men to move in on the station, he relayed that information to Annja and then began disconnecting the charging lines from the train's control center. Annja, meanwhile, took up a position near the bottom of the steps, the Russian rifle she'd confiscated in her hands.

Gianni, however, objected strenuously to waiting.

"We should get out of here," he said. "The tunnel ahead of the train is open, why can't we start walking?"

Annja looked at him for a long moment before saying, "We could, I guess, if we wanted to walk fifty kilometers back to Moscow. I don't know about you, but that's not high on my list of choices."

"Oh. Right."

He opened his mouth to say something more but never got the chance.

Screaming began to echo down to them from above.

THE PLAN WAS SIMPLE.

Assault the Metro-2 station with enough force and firepower to make it look convincing but leave Creed and company an escape route through the Metro-2 tunnels, which is really where Danislov wanted them to go, anyway.

Of course, with the tracker in place, Danislov could always pull his men back and wait for Creed to move forward on her own. But he guessed that Creed had come to expect a certain amount of tenacity from his unit and walking away now, when it seemed they had their prey cornered in the Metro-2 station, wouldn't look right. He knew from her dossier just how much that kind of thing nagged at her and how she would chase it down to find the truth. If she started to pull on that string, before he knew it she would have unraveled the whole thing, exposing Goshenko's hand behind it all. That would mean heads would roll, namely his.

No, better to stage the assault and get her driving forward toward the end game than to allow it all to grind to a halt right here and now.

It was a good plan.

And it fell apart not two minutes after it got under way.

The Metro-2 station had been built with only one way in and out—a single, narrow stairwell that led down a flight of steps to a simulated ticketing level and then down a second flight to the platform itself. There was no need for more as it was not intended to support the kind of traffic a real metro station saw on a daily basis, despite the fact that a working train did occasionally come and go.

That first, narrow stairwell created the perfect bottleneck and Annja had selected it as the location of her parting gift.

She'd taken care to string trip wires in an interlacing pattern halfway down the stairs, when those encountering them would be in the darkest portion of the stairwell. She arranged the mirrors along the walls themselves, using big sheets of stick-on Velcro to mount them. She even took the time to lay them out artistically at different heights and in different shapes so their presence might pass as decorative.

It was a simple trap and, as fate would have it, it ended up trumping Danislov's simple plan.

He sent his men down the stairwell in standard Russian wedge formation, guns out, night-vision goggles on, and his point man never saw the trip wires until he ran directly into them.

There was a click and a ping as the trip wires pulled the caps of the roadside flares she'd bundled together into little stacks, igniting them in a brilliant flash of white-red light that was picked up and amplified by the mirrors hanging in the small space.

For the men wearing the night-vision goggles, it was like staring into the sun as it went supernova from less than five feet away.

29

It sounded as if they were being skinned alive.

From her position at the bottom of the second set of stairs, Annja actually cringed to hear it. She'd meant for her pyrotechnic display to slow pursuit and hadn't really expected it to do much more than that, but judging from the noise she might have taken out some of those goons in a more permanent manner.

They've tried to kill you more than once, she reminded herself. They got what was coming to them.

She heard the train's electric motor cough into life behind her and turned to see Vlad hold up a hand.

Five minutes.

Should be easy enough.

Then the first bullets started to fly.

DANISLOV HADN'T STARTED down the stairwell when the trap went off, so he was able to squeeze his eyes shut and turn away at the first indication of trouble. That saved him from the worst of it.

His eyes still burned and watered, and he was stuck seeing stars for at least a minute afterward, but that was all. He pitied whoever it was who'd tripped the wire in the first place. They were going to be hurting for a long time. Hell, he'd be surprised if they could ever see again.

The men from the front rank were staggering back up out of the stairwell, helped by the others in the row behind who hadn't been as affected by the blast. The sight stirred vicious anger in Danislov.

What was wrong with this woman? Why the hell couldn't she just do what was expected of her for a change?

He felt the urge to smash something beneath his hands and took a couple of deep breaths to calm himself.

He'd scanned and loaded the blueprint for the facility onto his phone while aboard the chopper. He pulled it out and began paging through the files, looking for the one that covered the Metro-2 station. Finding it, he gave it a quick scan, nodded to himself and looked over to see which of his men were still able. After a moment's consideration, he called Subotin over to him.

"Come with me," he said, and the other man nodded.

They walked back to the stairwell and descended

one flight, kicking the still-burning flares out of their way as they went. When Danislov reached the bottom he stopped and looked carefully around the corner.

There was no one there.

He signaled to Subotin and then headed for the second stairwell. His subordinate followed at a respectful distance, not wanting to impede Danislov's firing arc if something were to go down.

Danislov could hear an electric whine coming from somewhere on the platform beneath them. He puzzled over that for a moment, before he realized what it was.

They've got a train.

Learning that the Metro-2 line was, in fact, real had been a shock, but any doubt disappeared the moment Goshenko had handed him the blueprint. Still, knowing the secret subway system existed and having an operational train that could take you down those tracks were two different things.

He wanted to see it for himself.

Danislov hurried to the mouth of the second stairwell. He had no idea how much longer Creed's party was going to be in the station. In his haste, he nearly received a bullet through the skull the moment he came into view.

He caught sight of a dark-haired woman kneeling at the bottom of the steps and of the long gun she was pointing in his direction, and then his instincts took over and he was hurling himself down and backward to escape the shot.

"Damn this woman!" he snarled as he picked himself off the ground.

It was time for this to stop.

If he had to cut off her fingers one by one to get her to take him to the library, he would. He didn't care about being subtle anymore.

Giving the staircase a wide birth, Danislov brought Subotin over to a metal grate set into a vertical pillar.

"This is a ventilation shaft. It starts on the floor below us and goes back up to the surface. While I distract the crazy woman, I want you to make your way down that shaft and wait for the right time to move in and subdue her."

A dark little grin crossed Subotin's face and for a moment Danislov considered asking someone else to handle the assignment, maybe Chechkov or Elanovin, one of the others who wasn't walking around with a chip on their shoulder the size of Red Square. But Subotin had a better chance of succeeding, with his long arms and legs.

"I need her able to answer questions, Subotin, so don't screw it up."

Between the two of them they made short work of removing the vent cover and then Danislov left Subotin to it as he returned to the stairwell.

This time he stayed back from the opening and simply shouted downward.

"Annja Creed!"

When he received no answer, he tried again.

"Annja Creed!"

He could hear his voice echoing down the stairwell.

"What?"

She sounded calm, in control.

"There's no need for all this foolishness, Miss Creed."

"I'm not the one who started it."

Danislov actually chuckled at that one. "I beg to differ, Miss Creed. You've got quite a list of complaints against you at the moment. Defacing and destroying a historical artifact. Resisting arrest. Assaulting an officer during the performance of his duties. Trespassing in a top-secret area. Shall I go on?"

He glanced over at the ventilation shaft but couldn't see Subotin anymore, so he knew he was on his way. Maybe another minute or two...

"Are you listening, Miss Creed?"

ANNJA STARED UP FROM the corner of the steps below, waiting for the cheeky bugger above to show himself again. She knew she was tired because he was starting to annoy her and that was never a good sign.

Patience, Annja, patience.

She knew he was stalling; there really wasn't any

other reason for him to talk to her. This wasn't a James Bond film where the villain unburdens himself of all the dastardly things he's done before killing Bond, allowing Bond, of course, to escape in the meantime. No, this was real life, and in real life the villain just shoots you dead.

Which he's already tried twice now.

But why? Why was he stalling?

That she didn't know.

She glanced around, but didn't see anyone else on the platform. She supposed someone might be making their way down the tunnel toward them at this very moment, but the platform lights kept her from seeing more than a few feet into the tunnel and there was no way she was going to hear them over the sound of the train's electric engine, so there was no sense in worrying about it until it happened.

Maybe they'd be out of here by then.

She glanced back to see Vlad and Gianni loading the recharged batteries back into the special compartments that housed them. They were big and bulky, making them awkward to work with and difficult to move. Vlad saw her looking and indicated it would take another three minutes.

Still? she thought. Damn!

"Are you still there, Miss Creed?"

She gave it a beat, then said, "My daddy always taught me not to talk with strangers."

She heard him chuckle. "I've been hunting you

for days, Miss Creed. I hardly think we're strangers to each other."

"Since you know my name it's only fair that you tell me yours," she called up to him.

She could sense him there, just beyond the top of the stairs, and edged forward, trying to get a better picture. His legs came into view from the ankles down.

"Sergeant will do, Miss Creed. Are you ready to discuss your surrender?"

"Surrender? Why would I do that?"

"You are not the only one caught up in this situation, Miss Creed. There are others involved, as well. I would hate for them to come to harm as a result of your unwillingness to be reasonable. What would Mrs. Vikofsky do, for instance, without her son to take care of her?"

Annja edged forward another inch. Now she could see him from the knees down. All she had to do was lean out a little more....

"Or that producer of yours back in New York. Doug, isn't it? New York is such a big, dangerous city that one could have an accident at any time...."

For just a second, the sergeant leaned forward, exposing more of his body to Annja. He was dressed in the same gray jumpsuit as the rest of his men. His hair was cut short, his goatee neatly trimmed, accentuating the scar on the side of his face rather than helping to hide it. He saw her at the exact same moment and his eyes widened with realization, but it was too late.

Yep, accidents happen all the time, she thought, and pulled the trigger.

30

For a moment she thought she had him. The shot was a decent one as these things go, but she had miscalculated the angle of the stairwell she was firing through and ended up missing him by about an inch, sending the shot flashing past his ear instead of taking him in the chest as she'd intended.

He cursed and pulled back out of sight, even as she sent two more shots flying in his direction, using the staircase wall to try to turn a ricochet into a lucky hit.

When she pulled the trigger a fourth time, the gun clicked empty.

"Time to go!" she said to no one in particular as she threw the empty rifle away, turned and ran for the safety of the subway car some twenty feet behind her. She could see Vlad and Gianni inside, urging her on. Apparently they were ready to get under way.

She had crossed half the distance, the open doors

beckoning to her, when something slammed into her with all the grace of a garbage truck.

Annja went down hard, scraping the side of her face against the unyielding surface of the platform as she bounced and slid for several feet with this weight on her.

The blow knocked the wind out of her and she was having a hard time regaining focus as she pushed herself into a sitting position.

The move helped clear her head and she realized belatedly that there was someone standing right in front of her. She glanced up, hoping to find Vlad or Gianni waiting to help her, but discovered instead the grinning face of the man she'd knocked out earlier that evening.

The fist he slammed into the side of her face told her he was still pretty pissed about it, too.

Down she went again.

With her head spinning from the blow, she barely noticed as her assailant picked her up like a sack of potatoes and hurled her across the platform to slam into the wall covered with ceramic tiles.

He'd underestimated her once and apparently wasn't going to make the same mistake a second time. Even as she was rolling over and trying to get to her feet, he headed back toward her, his movements swift and determined. Every facet of his being shouted, *It's payback time!*

Annja wasn't about to give up, though.

Should have stabbed him when I had the chance, she thought to herself, even as she scooped up some of the debris, dust and sand on the ground behind her with her right hand, using her body to shield the act from her assailant as he stalked toward her.

She waited until he was right on her, reaching for her again, before she went into action. She swept her right hand around and threw her handful in his eyes, causing him to rear back and howl. Annja used that opportunity to spin around and deliver the heel of her boot into the side of the man's knee.

He went back.

She scrambled to her feet just as the train let out a hiss of releasing hydraulics and jerked forward a foot.

They were so not leaving her behind.

She turned to move toward them when a hand grabbed her ankle in a viselike grip and yanked her off her feet.

Annja rolled over as soon as she hit the ground, not wanting to let her assailant get her into a chokehold and use his greater weight to end it. He apparently had the same idea, as he was pulling her toward him and trying to clamber up her body at the same time.

Out of the corner of her eye she could see the train starting to move, one inch at a time, rolling forward.

You need to be on that train.

She pulled back her free leg and kicked him in the face.

His head rocked back but he didn't let go.

She did it again.

Still no effect.

He batted her leg aside and with one heave pulled himself halfway up her body, pinning her legs beneath his torso. In another few seconds he would have her trapped beneath his larger, heavier form. After that, she would need a miracle to get free.

She twisted and turned, but got nowhere. He pulled himself astride her, one knee on either side of her waist, and reared up to deliver a hammer blow from over his head.

With no other options available to her, Annja manifested her sword and stabbed him through the chest.

His downward motion pushed the blade clear through him and he ended up staring right into Annja's face as he breathed his last breath.

She could hear Vlad and Gianni shouting now, could hear the train moving behind her, and knew, as much as she wanted to, she didn't have time to rest.

Annja released the sword and then heaved the dead Russian off of her. It was time to go.

31

Annja climbed wearily to her feet just in time to see several FSS agents in gray jumpsuits rush down the staircase, pistols in hand. She guessed they weren't all that happy to see her.

The feeling was decidedly mutual.

She didn't wait around to see what they wanted.

The train was picking up speed now, the long row of cars moving into the tunnel and farther away from her with every passing second.

Annja didn't stop to think, she just turned and ran for the far end of the platform, praying the last car would still be on this side of the tunnel mouth by the time she got there.

Annja took advantage of the element of surprise as the FSS agents were disturbed by the sight of the subway train leaving the station, and sprinted as fast as her weary body would allow after the train.

The sound was deafening as the guns echoed in

the confined space. Bullets struck the rear of the
train, ricocheting off the steel walls, shattering the
glass window in the door, even tearing holes in
the low fence that protected the short catwalk at the
end of the last car. Bullets whipped through the air
all around Annja but thankfully she wasn't hit. She
was closing in on the last car now, but knew if she
didn't pick up speed she wasn't going to make it.

Stopping the train, with the armed agents right
there on the platform, would be suicide for all of
them. Vlad and Gianni were leaning out of a window
farther along the train, shouting something back at
her. She couldn't tell what they said. It was lost in
the roar of the wind as the train sped up.

The bullets had stopped flying, as the gunmen
watched in amazement at what Annja was about to
attempt.

Annja probably would have been pretty amazed
herself if she'd had time to think about it.

Thankfully she didn't.

She was less than ten feet from the end of the platform and out of the corner of her eye she could see
the last car rapidly approaching.

Six feet...

Five...

As the front of the final car of the train passed by
her running form, Annja cut to the right and flung
herself out into space.

It seemed to her as if she hung in the air forever.

The train was still moving, still pulling away, as her body covered the last five feet in midair and she realized that no matter what happened, this was going to hurt.

With the blink of an eye, time resumed its normal flow and Annja slammed down onto the small catwalk, the final two feet of the car.

The force of the impact bounced her back into the air and she felt the g-forces snatch at her, trying to pull her back and away from the moving train.

She shot out a hand and grabbed the railing even as her body was carried over the edge.

That left her hanging off the end of the train by one arm, her body twisting to the right, threatening to tear her free from her precarious perch. She was scrambling frantically with her feet, trying to find some purchase and avoid getting them caught in the tracks at the same time.

Looking back, she could see the FSS agents standing on the platform, openmouthed and staring. As the train disappeared into the darkness of the tunnel, she was struck by the ridiculous urge to wave goodbye.

Then her hand slipped an inch.

"No. No, no, no, no!"

Another half inch.

The heel of one boot hit the tracks, bouncing her body back upward, and her grip loosened even more.

She fought against the wind and centrifugal force, trying to turn herself around so that her stomach faced the railing and she could grab it with both hands. But all she managed to do was slide even lower.

Only the first two knuckles of each finger were still wrapped around the bar and she could feel the aching strain on her wrist as the muscles were pulled tight.

Another few seconds was all she had....

A hand clamped down on her wrist, another grabbed her beneath the armpit and then Vlad was dragging her back over the gate and through the rear door into the subway car proper. They collapsed into a heap in a nearby seat. Her heart was pounding with equal parts fear and relief.

They stayed there, slumped together like that, for a long moment, both trying to catch their breath. When Annja was finally able to do so, she asked, "Who's driving this thing?"

That brought Vlad to his feet and sent him charging between cars back up the length of the train toward the conductor's compartment.

32

Annja remained where she was after Vlad left, content to just sit in the seat for a few minutes and try to compose herself. The massive adrenaline surge she'd been experiencing for the past two hours had finally peaked and she knew she was in for a hard dump on the other side as she tried to get her body back to equilibrium. Given the fact that she'd been squeezed, punched, kicked, thrown, shot at and nearly bounced from a moving train—all within the past thirty minutes, it seemed—it was a miracle she was still in one piece. Her body let her know it, too. She didn't think there was a square inch of her that didn't hurt.

The train rattled along on its slow but steady course and gradually the rocking of the subway car put her to sleep.

She awoke—it might have been minutes later, it might have been hours, she couldn't tell—to find Gianni standing over her, balancing himself by holding on to the handrails overhead.

"Vlad needs you up front," he told her.

She picked up on the strain in his voice and knew right away it wasn't good news.

"What's wrong?" she asked.

He told her it was best that she speak directly to Vlad.

Wearily, Annja got up and went in search of their resident expert on urban exploration.

As she moved from car to car, she noticed that the train was moving faster than it had been earlier. By the time she entered the conductor's car at the front of the train, she was convinced that it had sped up since she'd gotten up to move forward.

Was that even possible?

She very quickly discovered it was.

"We have trouble," Vlad said the minute she stepped into the car.

"What is it this time?"

"Train is speeding up. No way to stop it."

Annja digested that for a bit.

"You've tried to slow us down?

"Da."

"And it didn't work?"

"Nyet."

The train lurched beneath their feet. They weren't going dangerously fast yet, but if they kept up their current rate of increasing speed it certainly wouldn't be long before they blew past what she considered a comfortable rate of travel.

She glanced out the front windows, saw the walls rushing by in the lights of the train and suddenly had a near crippling thought.

What if there was a problem on the tracks?

The train hadn't been used in years. That meant the tunnel had most likely been left unused for that long, as well. Just about anything could have gone wrong in that length of time, from jammed track switches to collapsed walls and ceilings. They could be headed directly toward a cave-in right now and wouldn't have any idea that it was there until they ran straight into it.

"Can you just shut off the engine? Let it coast to a stop?"

"I try already. Either train malfunction in past and never fixed or else gunfire did something to controls. I cannot fix."

"So what are you telling me? We have to jump?"

A glance out the window showed them moving along pretty fast at this point. Jumping from the train at this speed would leave them smeared over the landscape.

"*Nyet.* We uncouple engine car."

Uncouple the engine car? While they were moving?

"Ah, okay. How do we do that? Just pull a lever or something?"

"If only it were that easy," Gianni said from behind them.

Annja turned, saw the expression on his face, compared it to the one on Vlad.

Whatever it is, I'm not going to like this.

"As far as I can tell from our illustrious leader here," Gianni said, jerking his thumb in Vlad's direction, "the tool that is usually used to uncouple the cars from the platforms between them is not on the train."

"Can we use something else as a substitute?" she asked.

"*Nyet*. Must be special shape to fit."

"But you said we need to uncouple the cars. How can we do that if we don't have this special tool?"

At least Gianni had the grace to look uncomfortable when he said, "You crawl underneath the car and manually disconnect it." Emphasis on the *you*.

"Ha, ha. Very funny," she said as the train sped up again on its own. "Now seriously, how do we do this?"

Neither of them said anything.

They weren't kidding.

Annja didn't know whether to laugh or cry.

"Why me?"

Vlad pointed at himself first, "Too big. No fit," and then over at Gianni. "Too *nyeuklyuzhii*." He flailed about, bumping into things, to illustrate what he meant.

Too clumsy.

A glance out the window confirmed that, no, they weren't miraculously slowing down all of a sudden.

If they wanted to get out of this with their hides intact, she was going to have to climb beneath a moving train and uncouple the engine car at high speed.

Great.

Just great.

Five minutes later Annja was stretched out on the small platform that connected the engine to the first of the cars. She stuck her head over the side, looking for the crank Vlad had described to her.

It wasn't easy. The ground was whipping by awfully close and every time Annja stretched out to try to look at the undercarriage she worried that her hair would fall forward and get snagged by something that zipped by beneath them. When she held her hair down with the strap of the headlamp she would be using and then bound her hair back with a bit of string they found inside the conductor's first-aid kit, she began to worry instead about the train passing over large obstacles on the track beneath it and getting struck by one on the way past. Of course there was no way to see such things coming, so…

"Ten kilometers left," Vlad muttered.

Annja whipped her head around to look at him.

He pointed out the window. "We just pass forty-kilometer mark. Ten kilometers until end of track."

Ten kilometers? At the rate they were going that left them…

"Grab the handle, crank it to the left six turns, push switch, right?"

"*Da.* Correct."

She checked the knot holding Vlad's climbing rope around her waist and double-checked that he was braced and ready to support her weight if she slipped. He gave her a thumbs-up and what he must have meant to be a reassuring grin. It was anything but.

She turned her headlamp on and slipped over the side of the platform before she lost her nerve.

33

The first thing she noticed was the sound. It had been bad up on the platform, a constant rattling hum that interrupted one's thoughts and made it hard to focus, but down here it was like a living force, pounding at her.

If she wasn't careful, the noise alone could get her killed.

It was slow going. There was about four feet of space between the underside of the subway car and the surface of the ground. That meant she had to hold her body up close to the underside of the rail car with the strength of her arms while jamming her feet into whatever footholds she could find and clenching her legs to keep them in place. In that fashion she moved, inch by inch, toward the hand crank. She had seen it from above, but now that she was down here everything looked different.

It was darker, for one thing, and even with the headlamp she had a hard time seeing. The occasional lights running the length of the track would flash through the openings in the wheels, creating a strobe effect that made it even more difficult to pick out what was solid and what was shadow. Twice in the first five steps she reached for what she thought would be a good handhold only to have to pull back when she discovered there was nothing there.

The rope tied about her waist kept getting caught on things, as well, and she would be forced to hold on with one hand while using the other to try to shake it loose. She thought about calling her sword and cutting it loose, but she knew the sight of the suddenly severed rope would make the other two think she'd been swept off the underside of the train. Heaven only knew what they would do at that point. So she kept at it, inch by inch, until she could see the white painted wheel with the hand bar jutting down from it only a few feet away.

Sweat was dripping into her eyes, but she just blinked it away and did her best to focus on the task at hand. She repeated the procedure in her head—six turns, counterclockwise, to prime the coupler and then a press of the switch to break away.

Sounded downright simple, really.

She should have known better.

The crank wouldn't turn.

She braced herself as best she was able, got a better grip on the crank handle and tried to get it to move.

Nothing.

Cursing a blue streak, which she couldn't hear over the noise of the engines, Annja carefully turned around and jammed her hands and feet into new holds to support her while she used one foot to kick at the crank.

All she got out of that was a sore foot.

What she needed was a lever.

She could use that to pop the crank free and hopefully release the coupler in time.

Miracle of miracles, she had just the thing.

Annja summoned her sword. The long blade shimmered in the light of her headlamp. She pulled her arm back, preparing to slide it between the sections of the wheel that formed the main part of the crank, when the train bounced over something on the tracks and Annja lost her grip.

The sword flashed once and was gone, swept away beneath the train.

Annja felt herself slip and it was only an instinctual grab for something sturdy that kept her from being swept away right after it.

She needed a few seconds to catch her breath after that.

She felt Vlad yanking on the rope, three quick tugs, which was the signal they'd agreed on as a way for Vlad to check in with her and see how she was doing.

Annja tugged back, twice, short and sharp.

Even better when I get myself topside again.

Annja summoned the sword again, knowing it would be there, waiting for her in the otherwhere, just as it was each and every time she reached for it. It didn't matter if it had been hurled off the deck of a ship, kicked over a cliff, buried beneath an avalanche of snow or dropped under a speeding train, the sword would always return to serve her.

On the day it didn't, she suspected she would no longer be worthy of wielding it.

This time she managed to slide the sword into place through the crank wheel and then put her weight on one side, using the sword blade as added leverage. Slowly, millimeters at a time, the wheel began to turn.

Using the sword, she moved it through a quarter rotation before testing it and discovering that it was loose enough to move by hand. At that point she let the sword vanish and grabbed the wheel's handle with her free hand. She cranked it as fast as she dared through six revolutions, then reached out and punched the switch with the palm of her hand.

There was a sharp crack as the coupler split apart and the two cars were suddenly free of each other.

Annja didn't wait around to see what happened after that. The muscles in her arms and legs were shaking, filled with lactic acid from all the climbing she'd been doing. If she didn't get back now, she might not be able to get back at all.

It would be the height of irony to succeed in the mission only to fall under the train a moment after.

As she crawled to the edge of the car, Vlad and Gianni reached down and hauled her up onto the platform. She rested a moment and then moved through the door into the car proper.

A glance through the window showed the engine pulling away from them. No longer hampered by all the additional weight at its back, it had begun to pick up more and more speed and before long it would be out of sight somewhere up ahead.

Vlad began applying the emergency brakes to slow the rest of the train until it finally came to a stop some fifteen minutes later.

From there, they would have to walk.

34

As it turned out, the train had come to rest three kilometers from the end of the tunnel. Annja knew this because she'd counted every step they'd taken down the tunnel, needing to know just how close they'd come to being splattered across the landscape.

Splattered was a good word for it, too. By some miracle the train's engine had never left the tracks. It had hurtled into the solid rock face at the far end. They had begun finding small pieces of the wreck at least a kilometer earlier and could only stand in stunned silence at what was left.

Even the larger pieces were difficult to recognize as having once been part of a train.

Vlad guided them past the flaming wreckage and up onto the station platform nearby, where a whale reached out and tried to kiss Annja.

Or at least that's what it seemed like to her. The mosaic covering the back wall of the station platform showed an enormous humpback whale breaching the water. It had been created with such artistry and skill that it gave the viewer the sense that the whale was moving toward them, stretching out of the surface of the wall.

It was exquisite and Annja felt a pang of sorrow that it was hidden down here in the dark.

Vlad caught her staring.

"Academy of Oceanography," he said, indicating the double doors leading off the platform. A change came over his expression. "Hall of Experimentation."

Hefting his gear, he led them inside.

Within moments it was apparent to Annja that the mosaic was some witty designer's way of trying to put lipstick on a pig. The Academy of Oceanography's vaulted Hall of Experimentation was little better than a workshop of horrors. It had been more than forty years since the facility had been operational and much of the interior had been cleaned out, but even from what was left Annja could see that the normal measures of oceanographic study were far removed from what had gone on here.

They passed through a massive preservation room that still contained a number of specimens in oversize jars of formaldehyde, floating in their tanks. The lights of their headlamps reflected off the glass and created the illusion that the specimens were moving inside the tanks, turning the place into a carnival sideshow of creepiness.

Annja couldn't wait to get out of there.

According to Vlad's information, there was supposed to be an exit to the tunnels inside one of the back offices. Sure enough, they found a gaping hole knocked into a wall at the exact location indicated. Vlad stuck his head inside the tunnel, looked around and pronounced it "Perfect."

Given what they'd experienced so far on their search for the lost library, Annja was starting to believe that "perfect" was a code word for "brace yourselves." But she was more than happy to leave the Academy of Oceanography and all its strange specimens behind. Even the grime of a three-hundred-year-old tunnel seemed preferable to that.

35

They fell into the same pattern they'd established underground previously—Vlad in front, sniffing out the trail, Annja in back, protecting the rear, and the less experienced Gianni in the middle.

Vlad was still working from his notes, the recollections of a close friend who was no longer with them, he confided, and so the going was steady but slow. The tunnels were an odd mix of eras, from the brick-lined passages put together by Catherine the Great's work crews to the steel-reinforced corridors that were filled with the detritus of the Cold War.

They had been walking for half an hour when they emerged from an earthen tunnel to find themselves standing in the middle of a corridor that reminded Annja of a supersecret laboratory straight out of a cheesy science-fiction flick. A series of reinforced steel doors on either side of the corridor were arranged in a staggered sequence. Each had a thick plate-glass window set in it. In those cheesy movies, the windows were to allow whatever was on the opposite side to be viewed from the corridor without opening the door.

Vlad barely noticed, but Gianni couldn't resist satisfying his curiosity. He edged up to one of the doors, looked through the window and promptly recoiled, hurrying down the hall in Vlad's wake.

After witnessing Gianni's odd reaction, Annja stepped up to see for herself.

It didn't appear all that extraordinary to her. Just a lab workroom, like any other, though one that seemed to have been suspended in the sixties. An old rotary telephone hung on the wall near the door and Annja noticed that there was a corresponding space for one on her side, too. Lockers lined one side of the room, a wooden bench bolted to the floor in front of them and she could see an old-style chemical protection suit hanging in one of the lockers that was open.

Then she saw the corpse.

He sat in a chair in front of a steel desk on the far side of the room, his head tilted forward on his chest as if he'd fallen asleep. His face and flesh had shriveled so badly that he looked like one of those shrunken-head dolls during Halloween. On the table in front of him was an open container half-full of strange blue crystals. A pile of those same crystals sat on the table in front of him.

Accident? Suicide? Annja couldn't tell.

She understood Gianni's reaction, though. There was something very unsettling about the scene, a sense of catastrophe only narrowly avoided.

She intentionally did not try the handle, then hurried to catch up with the others.

Farther down the tunnel they encountered a series of seven chambers, each once covered entirely with painted murals that shouted of a time and an age long passed. Blue guitars danced beside red mushrooms through a field of musical notes, rainbows and unicorns, smiling sun faces, even slogans like Groovy and Peace and I Love John Lennon.

The lights on their headlamps grew a bit dimmer and Vlad made them stop to exchange their old batteries for new ones. They took the time to drink some water, as well. Staying hydrated was important, they all knew.

After a five-minute break they continued.

Just a few more minutes brought them to the entrance of a bunker that must have been able to hold at least three thousand people. The sight of it put a smile on Vlad's face.

He pointed to the rock above their heads. "Cathedral of Christ the Savior. Destroyed by Bolsheviks in 1930s. Very close to destination now."

Ten minutes later the tunnel opened up before them, revealing three new passageways. Only one of them showed up on the map. Because it was hand-drawn and therefore not to scale, they didn't know which of the three the map depicted.

It was as good a reason as any to call a rest break. The three slumped to the ground, weary after the long hike through the tunnels and battling giant Russians and speeding trains. Annja sipped from her water bottle as she studied the three routes.

Her first inclination was to take the middle one, but that was just human nature, a built-in need to make everything even, to have it all be balanced in the end. Neither of the other two routes looked noticeably different, however, and it was going to be difficult choosing between them.

That's when she saw it.

Over the entrance to the tunnel someone had carved a crude representation of a dog's head next to a broom. She had to squint to see it, and she might have passed both carvings off as a trick of the rock, a result of natural formations rather than intentional design, if it weren't for what she knew of Ivan's secret police. Often called the "Czar's Dogs," they'd used the severed head of a dog lying next to a broom as a symbol of their strength and omnipresence.

Annja got up, poured a little water on her hand and wiped down the symbols. With the dust forced out of their grooves, the shapes stood out in stark contrast to the rest of the rock.

"Good, Annja!" Vlad cried, staring up in delight at her cleverness.

Annja was rather pleased with herself, too, truth be told. Fioravanti and his crew probably knew the tunnels well enough after a few weeks to move about without the help of any kind of markers. But she remembered from Fioravanti's journal that Czar Ivan had assigned squads of the Oprichniki to watch over the crew as they got close to the end and being underground had probably frightened them considerably. Not wanting to get lost in the maze, some enterprising Oprichniki soldier had clearly carved a symbol over the mouth of the tunnel.

"If my instincts are right," Annja said to the others, "we should have circumvented the cave-in at this point and reconnected with Fioravanti's original route. We shouldn't be far from the location of the vault. Not far at all."

Before anyone could respond, armed men rushed out of the darkness and surrounded them.

36

Vlad tried to resist but quickly had his feet kicked out from under him and a gun shoved in his face. That was enough to keep them from resisting further.

The newcomers were dressed in just the same fashion as the armed men they had encountered back at the former KGB training center in Ramenskoye. Annja wasn't surprised to see their scar-faced leader emerge from a nearby tunnel seconds after she and her companions were secured.

What was surprising was the fact that he was accompanied by an older man who appeared to wear a colonel's decoration.

The newcomer wasted no time in getting down to business.

"Ah, Miss Creed. So good to make your acquaintance," he said in a voice that reminded Annja of the snake-oil salesmen she'd encountered in the Quarter when she was a young girl in New Orleans.

"Allow me to introduce myself," he said in faultless English. "I am Colonel Viktor Goshenko of the Russian Federal Security Service."

Without waiting for her reply, he turned and indicated with his outstretched hand the scar-faced commando she'd tried to shoot in the underground facility in Ramenskoye. "And this is Sergeant Danislov, who I think you've already met."

Goshenko ordered the captives to their feet and, given the number of guns that were pointed in their direction, they chose not to argue.

"I understand that one of you has a map," Goshenko said. "If that map were to be handed over to me without argument in the next thirty seconds, I would guarantee you could walk away from here with your lives intact. Provided, of course, you never speak of this again."

Vlad said something in Russian, which Annja didn't catch. But apparently Danislov did. It must not have been flattering, because the sergeant wandered over and kicked Vlad solidly three times in the ribs. With all those guns pointed at him, Vlad had no choice but to stand and take it. If he tried to fight back, they most likely would have shot him on the spot.

Goshenko calmly waited until his henchman was finished, then addressed the captives once more. "No takers? Are you sure? We're going to find that map, anyway, one way or another."

Annja didn't like the sound of that, but still, she wasn't about to admit that she even knew what he was talking about, never mind give up the map.

How the hell did he know it existed in the first place? she wondered.

She found the answer to that in the next moment when Goshenko turned to Gianni and asked, "Who has the map?"

Gianni pointed to Annja. "She does. Would you like me to get it for you? I know exactly where she keeps it."

Annja could only stare at him. He must have been feeding them information all along, which would explain how they knew to come looking for them at the hotel and then again down in the tunnels beneath the university. Even while Annja and Vlad were plotting an alternate route to get to the treasure, Gianni must have been filling his superiors in on their plans and preparing to have them intercepted.

Like now.

"Turn the library over to the people of Russia?" Gianni mocked. "Are you insane? Do you think I went through all the trouble to get that windbag Davies on board to finance this search only to allow you to come along and let it all slip through my fingers? There are buyers who would pay millions just for a single book from that library, never mind several major volumes."

Gianni turned away in disgust and looked back

at Goshenko. The colonel shook his head and then advanced on Annja.

"We have two options at this point," he said softly. "Option one. You can give up the map of your own accord. Or two, I can order my men to hold you down and search you until they find it. I assure you the first will be far more pleasant than the second."

With no real choice before her, Annja gave up the map.

Goshenko, Danislov and Gianni moved just inside the entrance to the next section of tunnel to study it, leaving Vlad and Annja surrounded by several armed guards.

They tried to talk to each other at first, but one of the guards threatened to club them into unconsciousness if they didn't keep their mouths shut.

That didn't stop them from communicating, however.

Vlad looked at her once, pointedly, then stared for a moment at the set of guards standing a few feet away from her. He looked at her again to make sure she was watching, then glanced down at himself once before looking over at the guards standing close to him.

The message was simple enough.

We're getting out of here. You take out those guys over there, I get these guys over here, and then we'll deal with whatever happens next.

Annja thought it was a marvelous plan.

If they could find a way to make Gianni pay for his treachery in the process, it would be even better.

Vlad had no intention of waiting around for the perfect moment, it seemed. After glancing at the tunnel entrance, he surged to his feet, roaring like an enraged grizzly bear.

Given his size and strength, Annja thought that an apt description, indeed. Their captors hadn't bothered to secure them in any way, perhaps believing that two unarmed people would never be stupid enough to attack armed personnel. That proved to be a big mistake, as Vlad was up and moving before they could respond.

Vlad was looking to cause as much pain and misery as he could before they managed to cut him down. He started with the man standing the closest to him, lifting his foot and driving the tip of his steel-toed size-thirteen boot directly between the guard's legs.

The man hit the ground like a sack of rice.

Vlad was already moving forward, reaching out with those big mitts of his and slamming the next two men's heads together with a resounding crack.

Two sets of hands were always better than one.

Leaping up, she lunged toward the nearest of her captors even as she called her sword to hand. That first man died before he realized what was happening, as Annja buried three feet of tempered steel into his chest.

She snatched the man's gun from his hand as he was falling beneath her attack, shouted, "Vlad!" and tossed it underhand in her partner's direction. Then she was too busy dealing with two more of the Russian soldiers to see what happened next.

The sudden appearance of a broadsword in her hands had shocked the guards immobile for a moment. But now their minds were catching up with what their eyes were telling them and their hands were starting to obey commands. Namely, "Shoot her!"

Lucky for Annja the men's tactical discipline was poor. They had been standing bunched together in a tight little group, which made it easier for her to deal with them swiftly before they had time to bring their deadlier weaponry to bear.

After tossing the gun to Vlad, Annja dove forward, releasing the sword as she went, tucking her body into a ball and crossing the distance between her and the next gunman. He was still trying to track her when she came out of her somersault on one knee, swinging her arm around, the sword once more in hand.

The blade caught the second gunman under the ear and continued all the way out the other side of his neck with only a moment's hesitation when it encountered his spine.

But the third man was going to be more difficult. He was backing away as he brought his gun up, increasing the distance between them, and there was no way Annja could get to him before he could line her up in his sights. The smile spreading across his face indicated that he'd realized this, as well.

Annja brought her sword back over her shoulder and whipped it forward, sending it speeding through the air to drill itself through the back of his throat, cutting him off in midshout. With his spinal column severed, there was nothing he could do but bleed out on the floor at her feet.

Gunfire erupted behind her and she turned to see Vlad exchange shots with two of the other Russians from Danislov's group. She knew the moment a bullet from one of the enemy's weapons winged him in the hip, when he grunted and sagged slightly on that side. But that didn't stop him from bringing up the weapon Annja had tossed him and putting down both men with short bursts of controlled fire.

That's when Danislov came stalking across the room, pointing his gun at Vlad's unprotected back.

"No!" Annja screamed as she charged forward, trying to intercept what was coming but knowing in her heart that it wouldn't make a difference. That she'd never make it in time.

Her scream brought Vlad twisting about and his eyes widened as he saw who was coming toward him across the empty space of the room.

The weapon in Danislov's hand went off three times.

The gunshots had a nasty, final sound to them, or at least it seemed that way to Annja as she watched each of them unerringly find their target.

Vlad.

The bullets punched into his chest, jerking him backward with each blow as blood fountained into the air.

Twenty-five feet.

Twenty.

Danislov's attention was still on Vlad as he crumbled to the ground.

Fifteen feet.

Twelve.

Now!

She leaped, the sword drawn back over her head, ready to come down in a savage blow, a scream of rage bursting from her mouth.

Almost casually, Danislov swung his arm about and pointed the gun in her face.

The open barrel seemed impossibly large right up to the moment Danislov pulled the trigger.

37

Annja Creed fell in an ungraceful heap at the feet of Sergeant Danislov. Goshenko's man stood there, arm outstretched, gun pointed at the Creed woman's head, but he didn't find cause to use it again. She didn't move.

"Nicely done," Goshenko told him as he stepped into the room, genuinely pleased to have such a difficult individual as Creed silenced at last. He thought for a minute of having her body brought topside, possibly even paraded as a spy, but decided against it. It was too much work and might raise too many questions about what she'd been doing down here in the tunnels. No, better to just dispose of her and that pain-in-the-ass self-stylized explorer Vikofsky down here in the dark. Where the only thing that might ever stumble on them would be the insects that ate their decaying flesh.

The colonel watched as Danislov bent over the

woman's body. At first he thought the other man was feeling for a pulse, but then he came away with something small and red in his hand. He passed it to Goshenko.

It was the tracking device the traitor has slipped onto the back of her fireman's jacket hours before during the confrontation in the old KGB training center. Working with Travino had been a smart move. There was no way any of his men could have gotten close enough to plant that tracker on Creed, and without it they wouldn't have been able to hang so far behind them through the tunnels.

Danislov slipped the locator into his pocket. But he must have felt Goshenko's gaze on him, because he glanced up suddenly and nodded once in respect. Goshenko did the same in return.

Beside him, the Italian was engrossed in the map.

"I trust you know how to get us to the vault," Goshenko said. "Especially since the good sergeant just gunned down your competition."

"Of course I do," the other man sniffed. "I'm the one who discovered Fioravanti's journal in the first place."

Goshenko didn't care if Fioravanti himself had told him where the vault was buried as long as the Italian could take him there. The colonel hadn't doubted Creed's abilities, but this idiot...

He shook his head. He'd deal with that when the

time came, he supposed. For now, he wanted to get them under way.

First, though, they needed to get rid of the bodies. He sent one of Danislov's men out into the tunnels to find a suitable dumping ground while the others searched the bodies for anything that might identify them.

Good riddance, he thought, watching his men pick over the bodies of their former comrades. Anyone dumb enough to get themselves killed by a pair of unarmed captives was too stupid to live.

Except they weren't really unarmed, were they?

When he'd first heard the commotion he thought he'd seen something flash in the Creed woman's hand, but it wasn't until he observed that final showdown between her and Danislov that he realized what he was looking at.

The bitch had been wielding a sword that was at least as long as his arm, perhaps even longer.

Where the hell had it come from?

And perhaps more importantly, where had it gone?

The man he'd sent off to find a good place to dump the bodies came back, talking about a sunken chamber that was already full of skeletons. Goshenko forgot about the sword Creed had been using and focused on more important matters.

Like finding that library at long last.

38

Annja sat up with a gasp, her breath exploding out of her as if she'd just been punched in the gut. Memories flashed in her mind's eye—Gianni's contempt, Goshenko's gloating, the scar-faced Russian raising his weapon in her direction, the half mad, half desperate charge she'd made across the room, hoping to reach the gunman before he could pull the trigger....

In that moment she'd found out just how fast she actually was.

Not fast enough.

And yet, here she was.

Wherever the hell "here" happened to be.

She was in utter darkness. She couldn't see a thing—not even when she held her hand directly in front of her face and waved it back and forth. She reached up toward her forehead, looking for the headlamp she'd been wearing before she'd been shot.

It was gone, perhaps ripped away by the force of the shot, perhaps stripped from her after she was down.

Fear gripped her as a new notion occurred to her. What if she wasn't in darkness at all, but that she had lost the ability to see? Her head pounded like a steel drum and her stomach roiled with nausea, so it wasn't that much of a stretch to think she'd been blinded. It was a distinct possibility, as she was certainly experiencing the symptoms one might expect.

She heard someone whimpering and she went still, listening closely. When she didn't hear it again she breathed a sigh of relief, and in doing so realized she had been the one making that forlorn sound. That worried her even more.

It wouldn't do to survive getting shot in the head, only to succumb to madness.

Condition, then situation, she reminded herself, going through the litany she'd learned years ago during an Outward Bound course the nuns had sent her on in an attempt to quell some of her restlessness. The instructors had taught her that in an emergency, you had to understand the state you were in before deciding on the best way of extricating yourself from the situation. That your physical condition might limit the options available to you.

Condition, then situation.

Tentatively Annja reached up with her left hand and touched her temple. A bolt of pain shot through her head and her hand came away sticky with blood.

She gritted her teeth and did it again, this time moving her fingers farther back along her skull. Same results.

The bullet had burned a furrow down the side of her head, just below the hairline. A half inch to the left and she would have ended up with a gaping hole in the back of her skull instead. The wound hurt, a lot, and Annja worried that it had done more harm than she knew right now, that some vital connection to something—her eyes!—might have been damaged from the impact alone. She had little doubt the nausea and loss of equilibrium were a result of the injury, as well.

The good news was that the rest of her seemed intact and that she was relatively mobile. She might not be able to see her hands moving right in front of her, but she was confident that they were responding to the signals her brain was sending them because she could feel them. The same went for her legs.

To prove the point, she drew her legs up underneath her and rose to a crouch. She stretched her hands out on either side, the tips of her fingers balancing her against the surface she'd been sitting on, which turned out to be cold and slightly damp stone.

As she began to think more clearly and her fear receded, she began to put two and two together. Stone beneath her feet, complete darkness all around—it seemed likely that she was still underground, perhaps even in the cavern where she'd been shot. She felt the urge to call out, to see if there was anyone nearby. If the Russians, who no doubt thought she was dead, heard her, they would come back to finish what they had started. Without the ability to see, she would be unable to defend herself.

So, no shouting, then.

Instead, she ran her hands along the stone surface, looking for anything that might be of help to her. When she didn't find anything, she got down on her hands and knees and inched forward, still searching, not knowing what she would find. She was somehow more afraid of not finding anything at all, afraid that the darkness would just go on and on, that she would wander down here for weeks until she took a wrong step and ended up at the bottom of a deep hole from which she couldn't escape.

The feel of flesh beneath her fingertips caused her to recoil violently. That in turn impacted her hard-won equilibrium and set her head pounding even harder. She fought the urge to vomit and waited for her head to stop spinning before trying again, reaching out tentatively with one hand, hoping like hell the body was still there, that it hadn't gotten up and moved.

Her fingers touched dead flesh again and this time she successfully controlled the instinct to recoil. Gritting her teeth, she felt around in front of her with both hands, ignoring how she felt about touching the cooling flesh and the half-dried viscous fluid she knew to be blood. Given the man's size, it only took her a moment to recognize who it was.

Vladimir.

Annja bowed her head in grief. She'd genuinely liked Vlad. He didn't deserve what had befallen him. Even worse, he'd died in an attempt to save her life rather than his own. The world would forever be reduced from the loss of a man like him.

The world had too few heroes as it was.

After a moment she wiped the tears from her face, thought an apology in the dead man's direction and then put her squeamishness to the side and went to work. She checked the pockets of his fireman's coat first and hit the jackpot right away. The granola bar and bottle of water were excellent finds, no doubt about that, but when her fingers found the three-inch-long narrow plastic tube her heart began to beat faster.

She gripped the tube in both hands and tried to break it in two. It bent, just as she expected it to, and there was a soft pop from somewhere inside it.

Green light spilled from between her hands.

Annja decided there wasn't anything more beautiful in the world than a chemical light stick. She was relieved to know that there was nothing wrong with her eyes, that it had been only normal darkness that had kept her from seeing.

She raised the light stick above her head and looked around.

Vlad's corpse lay at her feet. The bullet that had killed him had struck him high in the neck, tearing out his throat and severing his carotid artery. He probably hadn't lived more than a moment after that, and for that Annja was glad. At least it had been merciful and quick. He was still dressed in the clothes he'd been wearing when she had last seen him. Apparently his killers hadn't had the time or the inclination to strip him of his possessions.

The glow of the light stick didn't reach much more than a foot beyond Vlad's corpse, but at the very edge of its light Annja could see his discarded fireman's helmet. On the helmet, affixed there with a rubber headband, was Vlad's spelunking lamp.

Annja scrambled over his body and dashed forward…only to come to an abrupt halt as she saw what was strewn across the floor at the far edge of the light.

Skeletons.

Dozens, if not more, of skeletons.

39

Annja put the light stick on the floor and picked up Vlad's fireman's helmet. There was no way she was going to be able to wear it over the wound on the side of her head, but she didn't care. All she wanted was the headlamp. Stripping it off, she set the helmet back down and then held the lamp near the light stick and looked it over.

It appeared intact except for a few nicks and scrapes. She found the light switch and with a silent prayer heavenward, she angled the headlamp away from her face and turned it on.

Light. Crisp, clear, white light. Annja felt immeasurably better. She had a little food, some water and light. It seemed she might get out of this, after all.

Holding the lamp in her hand, Annja stood and took a look around.

She was in a small chamber that was maybe fifteen feet across at its widest point. It had a low ceil-

ing and a sunken floor. The tunnel mouth was a
good six feet above it. She and Vlad were near the
entrance, right where she would expect them to be
if their bodies had been tossed from the mouth of
the tunnel. The bodies of the men she and Vlad had
killed during their abortive break for freedom were
stacked a few feet farther into the room, laid out with
far more respect than her own "remains" had been.

Past the more recent bodies, she stared at the dozens of skeletons, some still dressed in scraps of clothing, perhaps uniforms of some kind, that lay in the
rest of the room.

Annja moved to take a closer look.

They were all male, she could tell that immediately just by looking at the structure of the pelvic
bones. Their ages were harder to pinpoint. If she had
to say she would guess that they ranged from teen-
age boys to grown men, though she could easily have
been off. It would take a forensic anthropologist to
determine their exact ages; she was just making an
educated guess. She had no trouble identifying the
sword cuts and bullet wounds on the bones, however.
She'd seen too many of these marks not to recognize
them for what they were. These men had all suffered
a violent death at the hands of someone else.

What were the skeletons of murdered men doing
way down here? Then it hit her.

Fioravanti and his men.

She was looking at the remains of the crew that

had been brought in to build the vault for Ivan and then were slaughtered to keep the czar's secret.

Annja stared at them, stirred by their fate and their lack of a proper burial. It just wasn't right.

She vowed that if it was in any way possible, she would be back for them. She would see to it that the world knew what had happened to them, that their remains would be identified and given a proper burial. They wouldn't lie down here all alone in the dark for the rest of time if she could do something about it.

"I promise," she whispered.

She turned her attention back to her immediate need, which was to find a way out. Vlad's body had still been cooling when she'd touched it, which meant that it hadn't been long since they had been dumped here like so much discarded trash. The fact that they'd been treated so cavalierly made Annja's blood boil.

That, of course, brought the bastard Gianni to mind.

With the help of the light, she searched the bodies of the dead FSS agents, but didn't find anything useful. She then gave Vlad's body another once-over. She picked up his helmet and, after a moment's hesitation, placed it over his face. It reminded her of the way fallen soldiers were always treated in the films about World War II and that felt right somehow.

"I'll be back for you, Vlad," she told him, then,

with a final hand on his shoulder, she rose and moved to the mouth of the tunnel.

The opening was too high for her to pull herself up without help, so she stepped back and called her sword to her. Examining the area just below the opening, she found what she thought was a suitable place, then drew back her hands and jammed her sword deep into the earth at that point, creating a makeshift step. The activity sent pain shooting through her head, but she ignored it. If she wanted to get out of here, she didn't have any choice.

She leaned on the sword, trying to move it, but it was stuck in there pretty good, which was just the way she wanted it.

Annja backed up a few yards, shook her arms to psych herself up and then ran at the wall as fast as her beaten and injured body would allow. At the last second, she stepped up onto the extended blade of her sword and vaulted herself upward.

She grasped at the side of the entrance, scrambling for purchase. Her foot caught on a small ledge, giving her some balance, and she used that extra leverage, along with her arms, to haul herself up and out of the grave chamber.

Below her, the sword jammed into the cavern wall winked out of existence.

She was lying on the tunnel floor, catching her breath, when raised voices echoed back to her along the passageway from somewhere up ahead.

Discretion told her the best thing to do was to re-treat while she had the chance, to head away from the voices and search for a way out to the world above. She was vastly outnumbered and outgunned; even if she followed them, a confrontation made no sense. What did she hope to do against Goshenko and his men?

The enemy thought she was dead. They wouldn't be looking for her and so she would have the oppor-tunity she needed to get away from them, to find a way out without them hunting her through the dark passageways and tunnels.

But Annja wasn't listening to discretion. All she could think about was the way Vlad and she had been gunned down in cold blood, their bodies left behind to rot in some forgotten chamber deep underground. Or the expression on Gianni's face when he'd fin-gered her as having the map, clearly aware of just what the colonel had in mind for them.

She couldn't let that go.

Annja turned in the direction of the voices and quietly headed that way.

FROM HER VANTAGE POINT a short ways back down the tunnel, Annja could see into the chamber in front of her where Gianni and the FSS colonel, Goshenko, were arguing heatedly.

"I'm telling you, it should be right here!" her for-mer teammate was saying in English as she crept a little closer, the light of her headlamp off. Giving herself away was not part of the plan, after all.

Goshenko's contempt and annoyance were obvious even from this distance. Annja could see Goshenko's henchman, Danislov, off to one side, along with two of the other men they'd encountered earlier. The thugs had been pressed into service as light bearers, standing there holding bright halogen lanterns over their heads so the others could see the room.

The rest of the security team was missing. Either they were within a section of the room she couldn't see or else Goshenko had sent them off on another task, not wanting to share the moment of discovery.

Annja sincerely hoped it was the latter. That would make what she was about to do much easier.

The group stood within an intricately carved stone vault that looked as if it had been designed to hold the Library of Gold. Even from here Annja could see the swirl of colors from the Italian marble that made up the complex design covering the floor and the stone shelves covering the walls as far as she could see.

Except the shelves were empty.

The library, if it had ever been here, was gone.

"You told me you could lead me to the library," Goshenko said in a flat voice. "Where is it?"

Flustered, Gianni stalked over to a section of the shelves and began examining it closely, no doubt looking for some sign that the books had been here.

He pulled out the map, but he barely glanced at it before staring at the empty shelves around him again.

"It should be right *here!*" he said. "The map says so. Someone must have been here before us, must have smuggled the library out of hiding and moved it to a new location. That's the only explanation I can think of."

This time, Annja heard desperation creeping into his voice.

Gianni had seen what Goshenko had done to his former friends, Annja realized, and must now be having second thoughts about failing a man like him.

Annja wasn't shocked at all when it happened. Goshenko stared at Gianni a moment, as if weighing something, and then made a simple hand gesture to Danislov. As Gianni began to protest, Danislov smoothly drew the pistol from his holster and shot the Italian twice in the chest.

Gianni stood there for a moment, mouth open, and then toppled over. His blood splashed across the marble floor's beautiful surface.

Before the echoes had died, Danislov calmly walked over and put a third bullet through Gianni's head to finish the job. "When you told me the plan hinged on Travino, I warned it might come to this." He picked up the map that had fallen from Gianni's hands and gave it to Goshenko.

The colonel glanced at it, then tucked it away. He

headed toward the exit from the room, speaking over his shoulder to Danislov as the other man followed.

With Gianni dead, the two men had switched back to Russian, so Annja didn't bother to listen. Besides, if she didn't move, they were going to walk right into her, so she quietly turned and made her way back up the tunnel to where she had seen a small opening off to one side. She crawled into the space and pulled her legs in close, doing her best to make herself as small a target as possible.

She was just in time.

No sooner had she frozen in place than the light from the lanterns illuminated the passageway outside and the small group of men strode past. She'd been prepared to jump out and defend herself with her sword if need be, but thankfully the deep shadows kept her hidden from view.

She waited several minutes after they had left, then slowly crept out into the main tunnel. Her light was still off, leaving her surrounded by darkness, but this time she didn't mind. She looked in the direction the others had gone, but didn't see anything, not even a faint whisper of light floating back behind them.

Satisfied that they were gone, Annja turned toward the vault, flicked Vlad's headlamp back on and entered the room.

Unlike Gianni, Annja had plenty of experience with clever men who devoted their time and energy to devising hiding places for their sacred objects and treasures. She'd managed to defeat every obstacle such men had put in her path in the past and she was confident that she could do the same here.

Annja disagreed with Gianni's assessment. She didn't think the library had been smuggled away at some point in the past; she thought it was exactly where it was intended to have been. To rest through the ages.

The room they'd been standing in was a decoy.

40

Annja turned in place slowly, examining the room with intent. The chamber was an octagon, about thirty feet across. There were twelve shelves on each of the eight wall sections for a total of ninety-six shelves.

A lot of information had sprung up about the library over the years and, as with most other legends, Annja knew that the majority of it was complete crap. But sometimes there were kernels of truth mixed up in the legends. When it came to the legends, one of the pieces of information that continued to show up time and time again whenever the library was mentioned was that it was supposed to contain more than a thousand volumes. These were not slim volumes, either—certainly nothing like the average book you might pick up in any bookstore today—but rather thick, highly decorated volumes. Tomes, really. And as such they took up a lot of space.

There was no way a thousand volumes could fit in this small a space.

That was the first clue.

The second was the number of shelves.

Annja thought back to the clue they had discovered in the *Gospel of Gold,* the one that had led them to the map, which in turn had led them here.

2-6-8.

That's all it had said.

Which was why she found it so interesting that when multiplied together, those three numbers equaled the number of shelves in the room she was standing in.

Annja had learned long ago that there wasn't any such thing as a coincidence when it came to hunting for buried treasure.

Counting clockwise from the entrance way, she walked over to the second set of shelves and pushed down on the second shelf from the top.

Nothing happened.

She nodded to herself, then pushed down on the second shelf from the bottom.

It shifted slightly and clicked once.

"Gotcha," she said to the empty air.

She crossed the room, carefully stepping around the wide puddle of blood that had pooled beneath Gianni's corpse, and moved to the sixth wall section. She counted six shelves from the bottom, and repeated the procedure.

Shift-click.

Grinning now, pleased she had managed to figure it out without too much difficulty, she crossed to the eighth and final section. Counting up eight shelves she pressed down for a third time.

Shift-click-whir.

She could hear the rattle of a large clockwork mechanism as it unwound behind her. Turning, she gaped in surprise.

The center of the room had opened up in an iris, revealing the stone steps that led down toward the true treasure vault.

With her heart pounding in excitement, Annja began to descend.

41

The passage ahead of her was much narrower than any of the others she'd encountered so far in their search for the library. It wasn't wide enough for two people to walk abreast at the same time and that gave Annja pause as she prepared to step off the stairs.

Why create a passage so narrow? she wondered.

The answer, when it came to her, seemed obvious.

To keep your target within a specified area.

Annja went back up the stairs and out into the main corridor. She hunted until she found a rock about the size of a cantaloupe and took it with her back down the stairs.

Squatting at the edge of the last step, Annja rolled the rock down the length of the corridor. It tumbled end over end for a good ten feet before coming to rest in the middle of the passage.

It sat there. Nothing happened.

She shrugged, about to step off the stairs, when

the stone flooring beneath her makeshift trigger suddenly sank about two inches.

Annja barely had time to turn her face away and hug the wall for protection when the guns secreted along the length of the corridor went off with a vengeance. The sound was deafening. Musket balls came out of both walls simultaneously and Annja knew she would have been torn to ribbons if she'd been caught in that narrow space. As it was she was pelted with several razor-sharp chunks of stone that slashed her clothes and even drew blood from a nasty cut along one cheek.

When the cacophony finally stopped, Annja stood and surveyed the scene. She could now see a snake-like pattern of raised flagstones revealed on the floor of the corridor, all the rest having sank a few inches downward. Hidden rooms and pressure-plate traps. Her respect for Fioravanti's cleverness was growing.

So was her desire to go back in time and strangle the man.

SEVERAL HUNDRED YARDS DOWN the passageway, back in the direction from which they had come, Colonel Goshenko and Sergeant Danislov both stopped and looked behind them.

The sound of gunfire reverberated through the tunnel.

Without a word, they turned and retraced their steps to the empty treasure vault.

SATISFIED THAT THE PASSAGE in front of her was now free of obstacles, Annja stepped out onto the raised flagstones and made her way along the length of the corridor. What she found at the other end made her gasp in wonder.

A vast space opened up before her, this one even more beautifully adorned than the false library before. The floors were inlaid with bright marble that reflected her light back at her. The ceiling had been painted in traditional Renaissance style, the oil paints preserved so well in the dry underground climate, Annja imagined they hadn't changed since the day they'd been painted there by Fioravanti. The shelves were polished stone, fashioned right out of the living rock and spanning the entire circumference of the room.

But it was what those shelves held that truly captured her attention.

Books and scrolls and tomes of all kinds were lined up in rows, each one in its own special place. Gold and precious jewels gleamed back at her from hundreds of covers. The decorative additions to the books made them worth millions; the historical value of many of the texts made them priceless.

In the center of the room a single closed book rested on a pedestal all by itself.

Resolving to solve that puzzle momentarily, she turned her attention to the rest of the library. She was lost in admiring the collection when a voice spoke out of the darkness of the tunnel behind her.

"You are a difficult woman to kill, Miss Creed."

She'd heard that voice enough times now to know who it belonged to and she clenched her fists at the sound.

She slowly turned.

Colonel Viktor Goshenko of the FSS stood just inside the library, looking around in wonder. He had no concerns that Annja might try to hurt him, since his ever-present watchdog, Sergeant Danislov, stood beside him, staring at her all too eagerly.

"If you'd given him more time, he would have found it, as well," she said, referring to the recently deceased Gianni.

Goshenko focused on her instead. "I doubt that, Miss Creed. You were the one I was putting my money on, or didn't you know that? Surely you're smart enough to have figured that out?"

She was.

The colonel went on without waiting for an answer from her. "That fool Travino was just there as insurance, a way of making sure I got what I wanted in the end should something happen to you. You have no idea how delighted I am to see you alive and well. I was sorely disappointed when you startled us all by charging my man Danislov here and forced him to shoot you in self-defense."

Goshenko paused and his eyes narrowed as he

watched her closely. "Where did that sword come from, anyway?" he asked.

Annja didn't reply.

Goshenko cocked his head to one side. "What's that now? Cat got your tongue? You were more than happy to give your opinion a moment ago."

She ignored his comment. There was nothing to be gained by answering it and she certainly wasn't going to explain to the likes of him how she'd come by the sword or what it allowed her to do. Let him worry about it; it would keep him on his toes.

But unfortunately for her, Goshenko now had what he wanted—the Library of Gold—and saw no reason to keep her around. Without another word he signaled Danislov.

But Annja had seen that gesture before. Goshenko had used the same one to order Gianni's death less than a half hour before.

Even as the sergeant went for the gun on his belt, Annja was in motion, turning sideways to present a smaller target while at the same time whipping her right hand up behind her back as if she were getting ready to hurl a spear.

When that hand blurred forward a half second later, there was a broadsword grasped firmly in it, point forward.

Danislov was in motion, as well, turning and twisting to the left while bringing his gun up. He had it halfway to horizontal when she hurled the sword at him with deadly accuracy.

The blade entered his body just below his armpit and slid between his ribs to come out the other side.

He collapsed before he had a chance to fire a shot. From his stillness, Annja was confident he was dead.

The sword winked out of existence, only to appear a split second later back in Annja's hand.

Her battle senses were screaming at her now, shouting that she'd left the other opponent unobserved too long. That if he had a gun she was already dead....

She spun to the left, searching for Goshenko.

The bullet took her in the left leg, passing through the meat of her calf without striking anything vital but knocking her off her feet in the process. She yelped in pain even as she was rolling frantically to the left, trying to get out of the way of the bullets she knew had to be following.

More shots ricocheted off the marble behind her as she kept rolling, her mind racing, searching for a way out.

That's when she came up against the pedestal in the middle of the room and rolled to an abrupt halt.

The sudden silence in the room was broken a moment later by Goshenko's laughter.

Gritting her teeth in pain, Annja peeked out from behind the pedestal.

She didn't see him.

"Over here."

The voice was coming from behind her.

Fully expecting a bullet through the head at any moment, Annja slowly turned the other way.

Goshenko stood with his back to one of the shelves, his pistol pointed straight at her.

"On your feet," he said, and this time she could hear his anger.

The colonel, it seemed, had finally had enough.

Using the pedestal for support, Annja dragged herself to her feet, doing what she could to keep her weight off her injured leg and holding her head high. She might be caught dead to rights in the other's sights, but she'd be damned if she went out meekly.

Glancing down, she happened to note the title etched into the cover of the tome resting atop the pedestal.

Apocalisse.

It was Italian for *apocalypse.*

In all the literature she'd read on the Library of Gold, she'd never heard of a single book by that title, never mind one written in Italian.

Fioravanti! Oh, you clever devil.

42

"From the moment I heard your name I knew you'd be trouble," Goshenko said, staring at her with venom in his eyes. "You've been extraordinarily lucky so far, but this is where it ends. I've had enough of your meddling."

Goshenko took two steps forward and centered the gun on the bridge of her nose. The barrel loomed impossibly large in front of her, like a giant hole she was teetering on the edge of. One wrong move and she'd fall inside it forever. Vertigo washed through her.

"But I'm not done yet, Colonel," she told him softly and slammed her hands down on the cover of the book in front of her.

Goshenko fired.

Annja flinched.

That instinctive reaction saved her life. The bullet passed by her face with a subsonic crack and embedded itself into a thousand-year-old gold-laminated tome on the shelf behind her, missing her by less than half an inch.

Beneath the weight of her hands, the book sank down into the pedestal just as it had been designed to do whenever anyone touched it. It was the final trap designed by Gianni's ancestor, Ridolfo di Fioravanti, and it reached across the centuries to protect the one who had finally come to discover his fate.

The descent of the book set off giant clockwork mechanisms embedded deep in the walls behind the bookshelves. In every instance those mechanisms worked perfectly, sending a stone rocketing toward a piece of metal, striking a spark, which in turn ignited the kegs of black powder that had been standing there for centuries, just waiting for a light.

The resulting explosions tore through the stone shelves, sending earth, rock and the remains of priceless books in every direction.

And that was only the first wave.

Goshenko was standing right in front of one of the wall sections that exploded and even as Annja watched he was buried beneath a thundering pile of debris. She didn't wait around to see if he clambered back to his feet, however, for her attention was already on the rear wall, searching for that little detail Fioravanti had unwittingly revealed in his recounting of what happened on that last day.

I constructed an emergency tunnel at the rear of the vault....

Annja just hoped they hadn't filled it in again when they were finished with the construction.

She scanned the rear wall, conscious of time ticking down as the explosions continued. The whole room was shaking now and debris was falling from the ceiling, indicating its pending collapse. She had seconds at best....

There!

A three-foot section of the far wall collapsed inward, revealing itself to be plaster slapped over a wooden frame and painted to look like the rock around it. Beyond it, a narrow tunnel beckoned her.

Move! she screamed inwardly, and her body listened, scrambling to take her forward across the shaking and unsteady ground.

More explosions tore through the room, sending Annja crashing to the ground and this time she stayed there, choosing to crawl rather than fight the ground's shakiness from her feet. Especially with an injured leg.

She kicked and clawed her way forward, expecting at any moment to be buried, but somehow avoiding the worst of it until she reached the entrance to the emergency tunnel and threw herself in.

Behind her, in the center of the room, the ceiling

directly above the pedestal suddenly gave way, collapsing and bringing everything else with it.

The books!

Annja curled up against one side of the tunnel, drew up her knees and tucked her face into them with her hands over her head and rode it out.

The shaking and crashing went on for what seemed forever.

When it finally stopped, Annja cautiously raised her head and found herself once again shrouded in darkness. The headlamp she'd been wearing strapped to her arm had been smashed.

She was trapped in the dark.

But then she remembered the gear she'd taken off Vladimir and reached into her pocket for the light stick. She breathed a sigh of relief when she felt it.

The light it provided wasn't all that bright but it allowed Annja to take stock of the situation. She saw immediately that the entrance back into the vault had been blocked off by a cave-in similar to that which had buried her before. Going back the way she'd come was now permanently out of the question.

That left only the emergency exit tunnel for her to use and she wondered how Fioravanti might have felt if he'd realized, all those centuries before, just who might have need of the tunnel in the future.

She hoped he would approve.

Fioravanti's journal had said that the tunnel ran directly to the surface. She hoped that was true. The light stick would only last so long. She didn't want to be caught down here in the darkness without any light. That might just be the final straw that would do her in.

With the light stick in one hand and her sword in the other, Annja set out for the surface.

43

An hour later she emerged from the tunnel to find herself in the midst of the Bolshaya Pirogovskaya Street subway station. Several people stood on the platform waiting for the next train when she stumbled out of the tunnel, boosted herself up onto the platform and climbed the stairs. Her every move was watched, but no one tried to stop her or asked what she had been doing in a restricted area.

Once out on the street she hailed a taxi and asked the cabbie to take her directly to the nearest shopping plaza. He hesitated when he got a good look at her, taking note of the fact that she was covered with dirt and was wearing a filthy bloodstained bandage around her head and another around her leg. Anticipating his objections, she showed him that she actually had enough cash to be able to pay him when they arrived and that seemed to settle the matter.

She had him wait outside while she bought a

change of clothes in one store and a small bottle of Betadine and a first-aid kit in another. She then used the restroom to clean herself up. The cut on the side of her head wasn't all that bad; like any head wound, it had bled a lot but it wasn't that deep, and she felt considerably better once it had been coated with anti-bacterial ointment and covered with a wide bandage.

The calf wound was another story. The bullet had gone clean through, which saved her the trouble of trying to dig out a slug Rambo-style, but left her with a half-inch hole in her leg that was going to get rapidly worse if she didn't do something about it.

She had cleaned the area around the wound, so all that was left to do was deal with the wound it-self. Gritting her teeth, she put her leg up in the sink and turned on the cold water, letting it wash directly through the wound.

It hurt.

A lot.

After a few minutes she patted it gently with a cloth, then poured some of the Betadine directly into the wound. The iodine solution would help stop an infection until she could get the wound looked at by a doctor. She packed both sides with dry gauze, then wrapped the entire wound with tape.

When she emerged from the bathroom her hands were shaking but she looked considerably better, the cut on her head hidden beneath a bandanna, which in turn was covered with a loose-fitting baseball cap.

She'd noticed an internet café down the street upon arrival, so she paid the cabbie for his time and walked to it, slipping inside just as it opened for the morning. She got herself a hot chocolate and a pastry to provide some immediate energy, then paid for a half hour of computer time and the use of a headset/microphone combination. She took her food and gear to a station near the back of the room where she would still have some privacy once the café started to fill up. Then she logged in.

After checking that she had a decent connection, she downloaded Skype and used it to place a direct call to Sir Charles Davies's home telephone. He must have been waiting by the phone despite the late hour in the U.S. He answered it on the first ring.

"Are you all right?" was the first question he asked once he'd confirmed it was her who was calling.

He didn't ask about the library; he asked about her.

Annja realized she not only liked but respected Charles Davies. It made confessing her failure to him that much easier.

"No, I'm not all right. Neither are Gianni or Vladimir."

"Tell me what happened."

Annja did. She told him everything, including some of the things she'd left out the last time they'd talked. She told him about Gianni's treachery and of how he'd reported their whereabouts and discoveries to the FSS colonel, Goshenko. She described how Vladimir had died trying to give her time to escape when at last they'd been taken captive and how she'd had no choice but to leave his body down in the tunnels. She told him of the cleverness of Fioravanti's design for the library and how she discovered the final entrance to the sanctum of sanctums. How she'd seen the books that Ivan the Terrible had hidden away from the world and how, in the end, she'd been forced to bury it under a ton of earth and rock to keep it out of Goshenko's hands...and to stay alive.

It was a long conversation.

By the time she was finished, Annja felt as if a heavy burden had been lifted from her shoulders. Whatever happened now, she was ready to deal with it.

"I'd say it's time we got you out of there."

Annja agreed.

"I'll make some calls to someone I know over at the embassy. Give me half an hour and then head directly there. Ask for James Wiley when you arrive. He'll be able to get you a new passport. In the meantime, I'll book you a ticket on a flight back to New York. All you'll have to do is pick it up at the airport once you have your passport dealt with, understood?"

It sounded like a plan to Annja.

She finished her cocoa, then returned to the street

and hailed another cab. This one didn't give her any grief when she asked him to take her to the U.S. Embassy.

During the drive, her thoughts turned to the FSS colonel, Goshenko. She wondered how long he'd been in cahoots with Gianni, the two of them driven by their need to share in the millions they would get by selling the library on the black market. And what had originally brought them together.

She guessed that Goshenko had been working through unofficial channels, using the resources and manpower of his agency for his personal business. She'd begun to suspect that was the case long before she could even give the FSS colonel a name, when he'd just been a shadowy force chasing them for unknown reasons. Someone working the system properly would have issued arrest warrants and had the entire law enforcement community in Moscow looking for them. When that didn't happen, especially after she'd been forced to kill a man in self-defense inside the Marriott, she'd known something wasn't right.

At least now she understood how the FSS had tracked them down so many times. With Gianni to feed their position to Danislov and Goshenko, all they'd had to do was sit back and wait for Annja and Vlad to locate the library, then take it for themselves.

Her heart ached when she thought of Vlad's death. He'd been a good man, one who was as passionate about his work as she was about hers, and that was something she could understand at a deep level. She wondered who would take care of Mrs. Vikofsky now that Vlad was gone and made a mental note to see if Charles Davies could do something for her. If he couldn't, she'd find a way to get Roux or Garin to help her out. That old woman wouldn't be left alone, wondering what had happened to her son for the rest of her days.

Annja felt the car slowing and heard the cabbie muttering to himself in Russian. She looked up to see that they were just down the street from the embassy, the nine-story gold-and-white building looming over those on either side of it. But there appeared to be some kind of commotion. Several cars were parked haphazardly in front of the main entrance, their doors open, while men in dark suits were shouting and arguing with the marine guards standing there.

There were nearly a dozen cars in front of them, but traffic was at a standstill because of the commotion. Annja's driver put the car in Park and got halfway out, trying to hear what was being said. After a moment he got back inside, disgust on his face.

"What's going on?" Annja asked as a chill began to work through her bones.

"Security Service," he said, pointing at the men arguing ahead of them. "Looking for someone."

Annja rolled down her own window and looked

out, trying to get a better view. One of the men looked familiar....

The Russians suddenly stopped arguing and turned away. As they did so, Annja got a good look at their leader and froze, not believing what her eyes were seeing.

Despite the bruises that mottled his face, Sergeant Arkady Danislov was easy to recognize from the scar on his cheek. He was holding himself very stiffly, a result, no doubt, of the wound she had given him, a wound that probably would have killed nine out of ten men.

Apparently Danislov was made of sterner stuff.

He looked up then, his dark eyes taking in the cars stopped in the street, and for a moment Annja thought he had seen her. Bile rose in her throat and she trembled as she realized what this development was going to do to her chances of getting out of Russia without difficulty.

There was no way for her to get into the embassy now, not with Danislov and his men watching the front gates. She thought furiously for a moment, then turned to the driver.

"Forget the embassy. Please take me to the airport instead."

It took them nearly a half hour to get to the airport and by that time the cab fare had eaten up almost all of what little money Annja had. After paying him, she barely had enough to buy a decent meal;

hopefully she wouldn't be here long enough to need any more.

She entered the terminal, frantically trying to figure out what to do and constantly looking over her shoulder for the arrival of Danislov and his FSS goons. If they were even real FSS agents—for all she knew they were just mercenaries that Goshenko had recruited to help him with his dirty work.

Sir Charles Davies had sent her the ticket information by email and she'd printed it out before signing off in the internet café. She pulled the paper out of her pocket, found the proper airline and then printed out her boarding pass with the help of her record locator number.

Now she had a physical ticket, but the truth was that it was of little use to her since she didn't have any way to get past the security screen and over to the departure gate. One needed a passport for that.

She found an empty seat and sat down, taking the weight off her leg for a few minutes while she tried to work out a solution. She was having trouble concentrating, though; the longer she sat there the more she felt as if everyone's eyes were on her. She looked as if she'd been hit by a train, no doubt; she was obviously injured, and had no luggage, never mind what she was sure was a worried, possibly even frantic look on her face. She was a spectacle and she knew it. All she needed now was for some international *Chasing History's Monsters* fan to recognize her and throw her picture up on Facebook and her day would be complete.

International fan...

Annja lurched to her feet, the tiniest hope flickering in her heart. She began searching her pockets. "He gave me his card. All I have to do is find his card..." And then she remembered. She didn't have Yuri's card; it was back at Vlad's with her backpack and the rest of her belongings. These weren't even her clothes, for heaven's sake.

But that didn't mean the idea wasn't a good one. And there was more than one way to skin a cat.

She got up from her seat and began to move through the airport in the direction of the security screening area. She slowed as she drew closer, looking for one of those soft blue uniforms she'd seen that first night, the night she'd met Yuri after waiting around for what felt like hours in a windowless interrogation room.

Spotting one, she worked her way through the moving crowd until she reached the officer in question. It was a woman, tall and severe, with a pinched face and straw-colored hair that had been secured in a tight bun atop her head. She did not look happy at Annja's approach.

"Excuse me?" Annja said, trying to look as harmless as possible.

She must have succeeded because the immigration officer barely glanced at her. "Yes," the woman said, looking beyond Annja.

"I need to get a message to my friend, Yuri Basilovich," Annja began, trying to weave a story together out of thin air that might seem even quasi-believable. "I've lost my phone, my purse, even my ID. I know Yuri will help me if I can just talk to him. Please?"

She stared at the officer, begging her silently with her eyes.

"He's busy. You'll need to make a appointment," the officer said without looking at her.

That wasn't good enough. "Look, I'm sorry," she said, "but I really need to talk with Yuri. Can you just call him, please? Tell him Annja needs his help. Please?"

She didn't know if it was the begging, the tears in her eyes or her hand on the women's arm. But finally the officer saw her, really saw her, and that changed the picture entirely.

"Stay here," the officer said, and disappeared behind the secure area to, hopefully, hunt down Yuri.

She was gone a long time and Annja began to grow more and more nervous as she thought about what Danislov would do. He clearly thought she had survived; otherwise, he wouldn't have been looking for her at the embassy.

Annja had a good view of the entrance from where she was standing and right at that moment a group of sedans roared to a stop out front. Car doors were flung open, members of the public were pushed out of the way and Danislov and his men entered the airport.

Oh, no. Not now.

Danislov and his men spread out, began moving through all the passengers, checking faces.

She turned, preparing to run, heaven knew where—

"Miss Creed?"

Annja nearly screamed as a hand touched her shoulder from behind. She spun around, her own hand over her mouth so she didn't give herself away, and discovered Yuri standing on the other side of the caution tape.

His expression fell when he saw her. The black eye from her fight in the cavern, the bandage on her head, the stiff way she walked in an effort to avoid putting too much weight on her leg.

"Holy Mary," Yuri exclaimed. "What happened?"

At a shout from behind her, Annja cast a frantic glance over her shoulder. Danislov and his men were converging on a dark-haired girl about the same age as her.

She turned back to Yuri. "I can't explain right now, but I'm in trouble and I need your help. I wouldn't ask if it wasn't urgent."

He took a look over her shoulder and his expression hardened.

"Is that man looking for you?" Yuri asked.

Annja didn't hesitate. She had one chance at this and it had to work.

"Yes."

She had no idea what was between the two men, but her answer galvanized Yuri into action.

"This way," he said, taking her by the arm and leading her through the security area as her personal escort. Once on the other side, he unlocked a small office and ushered her inside, closing the blinds while she stood nervously watching.

Yuri faced her, his expression serious.

"Have you done something to harm my country?"

Knowing that everything hinged on her answers, Annja shook her head. "No."

"Does that—" he struggled to find the right word "—jackass out there have a legitimate reason to be chasing you?"

She shook her head, more confident now. "No."

Yuri nodded to himself several times. He said something in Russian too low for her to hear. "Do you have your passport?" he asked.

Annja shook her head.

"Ah! Now I understand. You want me to escort you onto your flight so that *ublyudok* out there does not find you."

Annja was stunned. She had hoped but... "Yes. Would you do that for me?"

Yuri beamed. "Annja. I am your number-one fan! Of course I will do that."

In the end, it wound up being rather anticlimactic. Yuri monitored the boarding process from the computer in the office and just before the plane was scheduled to depart he commandeered a hospitality cart and drove her directly to the aircraft. He had a word or two with the flight crew and pilot, then led her aboard the plane and put her in the only empty seat in first class.

"I don't know how to thank you enough," she told him.

He just laughed and patted her hand. "Someday you come back to Russia and tell me what happened. In the meantime it will be our secret and I will laugh every time I see that fool from FSS, *da?*"

She nodded. *"Da."*

The flight crew began preparing the cabin for takeoff and Yuri gave her a big hug before slipping off the plane. Annja spent an anxious half hour after that, expecting the aircraft to be called back at the last minute, praying there wasn't a mechanical or weather delay that would keep them on the ground.

It was only when they finally got into the air and the airplane effectively became U.S. soil for diplomatic purposes that she breathed a sigh of relief.

She must have fallen asleep for the duration of the

flight, because the next thing she knew the flight attendant was gently shaking her awake.

"Welcome back to New York," she said.

Annja smiled.

She couldn't think of anywhere else she'd rather be.

* * * * *